I0720408

PULLING UP STAKES

A CampCon Anthology

LEAH CUTTER   LAURA ANNE GILMAN

MANNY FRISHBERG   S. B. SEBRICK

GERALD NORDLEY   BRUCE TAYLOR

SANAN KOLVA   IRENE RADFORD

BOBBY LEE FEATHERSTON

Edited by
JOYCE REYNOLDS-WARD

Knotted Road Press

Pulling Up Stakes
A CampCon Anthology
Copyright © 2018 by Knotted Road Press
All rights reserved.
Published by Knotted Road Press
www.KnottedRoadPress.com

ISBN: 978-1-943663-72-9

Cover Art:

© Frank Rohde | Dreamstime.com - Futuristic eco wave background design

Cover and interior design © 2018 Knotted Road Press

This book is licensed for your personal enjoyment only. All rights reserved. This is a work of fiction. All characters and events portrayed in this book are fictional, and any resemblance to real people or incidents is purely coincidental.
No part of this book may be reproduced in any form or by any electronic or mechanical means, including information storage and retrieval systems, without written permission from the author, except for the use of brief quotations in a book review.

Introduction © 2018 by Joyce Reynalds-Ward

Better Places to Be © 2018 by Laura Anne Gilman

Mountain of Fire and Gold © 2018 by Sanan Kolva

Child of Two Worlds © 2018 by S. B. Sebrick

She Made Me Laugh © 2018 by Irene Radford

Made to Die © 2018 by Bobby Lee Featherston

Run, Lagomorph © 2018 by G. David Nordley

To Plant or Pull Up Stakes © 2018 by Joyce Reynolds-Ward

Euterpe's Song © 2018 by Manny Frishberg

The Ant Queen © 2018 by Leah Cutter

Franklin © 2018 by Bruce Taylor

Contents

Introduction

I've always enjoyed writing outdoors, whether it's been huddling next to a wood stove in a cabin wall tent with my late lamented Silver Reed portable typewriter, hanging out at a music festival with my tablet, or snatching moments between loading firewood into the pickup with my MacBookPro. So when I started going to Campcon, settling in to write under the mixed Ponderosa pine, lodgepole pine, and deciduous forest on the northeastern flanks of Mt. Hood just plain came naturally.

Over the years we've had plenty of adventures at Campcon, whether it be sweltering in mid-July heat, freezing in early June rainstorms, bee stings, or, at the 2017 Campcon, an incident which sent steaks flying through the air (all I've gotta say is that something that looks like it might serve as a campfire grill…may not be advisable to use as a campfire grill. No harm done in the long run).

I don't *know* for certain that this incident inspired the theme for this year's Campcon anthology, but I'm sure it had an influence. Nonetheless, we've got some excellent stories to serve up to you this year. No flying steaks, alas, but different looks at the theme of *Pulling Up Stakes*. Here you will find rootless spaceport denizens, women with purpose, magicians trying to prove their worth, alien visitors, gods and goddesses, genetically engineered creatures who just want to live a normal life, sentient aliens, and more.

Enjoy!

Better Places to Be

LAURA ANNE GILMAN

A Portside Story

"Stay safe," Josey's brother used to tell him. "Whatever you do, stay safe."

It had been a joke. There were no safe places in Portside.

Clean places, yes. Well-lighted places, yes. Populated places, many. But none of them were safe. Not if you lived in the creases. You made your own safety, tied yourself to as many kites as you could, built as many boltholes, and trusted none of them.

Someone hot had come in through the Port today. Nobody knew who, but it was all the whisper, jumping from mouth to ear. A muckwuck, higher than Admin. The gaming layers above the crease were off-limits to locals; spacers and Admin only, and if they thought they could bar spacers without the stores howling about lost sales, they likely would have.

Nobody cared about what happened in the market, though. Market was for crease and down-drifters, and contractors looking to slum it for thrills, or something they thought they couldn't find elsewhere. If there was money for it, Market had it.

Josey watched from his corner as the 'lifter disgorged its crew. Dreggi, Sassini, Human, all clad in black jumpsuits and slicks, moving silently, as though they had already used up their lifetime's allotment of words during their jumps between stars.

He was supposed to be down among them, working the crowd, listening and nipping what he could. But it wasn't safe. Not with security on alert, actually checking slips and looking at faces. If you were in the crease, you'd get lifted, and once you were lifted…well, people tended to disappear.

He cursed whatever muckwhuck whose visit had set security in a tither, and made his life harder.

It wasn't safe to go back without a day's work to show, either. Mather would have his hide on a wall.

He was, any way 'round, screwed—unless he could find a score that could make up for it….

Down in the crowd, Melichi stopped, his antenna flicking ever so slightly. "We are being watched."

"Everyone watches, Mel. Ship's Landing is the hour's entertainment." His companion was human, a woman almost as tall as the Sassini, but with more flesh on her bones. Still sparse, but then, Rhe claimed Sassini made famine victims look healthy. There wasn't much you could do with an exoskeleton.

"Someone specific," Melichi clarified. "Watching us specifically."

"Lovely." Rhe didn't look up, walking at the same steady pace as before. "You think they're after the skids?"

"Maybe." Likely.

His cluster-sister hummed under her breath, an annoying habit he'd yet to break her of. "You want to check it out?"

Mel exhaled, already knowing where this was going to lead. "Not really. But we should."

They were supposed to be couriering the skids in their bags to the client. No stops, no sightseeing, no side trips. But someone watching a courier was bad news, even if the watcher was innocent enough. They made a career out of not being noticed, blending into whatever crowd they were traveling with. It was easier than trying to fight every up-and-coming thug or assassin who had delusions of making a name for themselves by taking on a courier.

The only name those folk ever got was 'dead,' and killing people was a waste of the client's time.

They were under direction to deliver the skids to Admin Station, at the base of the Arcade. Instead, they turned left at the statue of Admiral Peasquank, passing the Sasqueeha Medical Center, with its courtyard of void amputees being treated with artificial sunlight. Rhe gave the old spacers a salute, then jerked her chin at the crowded mass of Market Street, a colorful squalor of stalls and storefronts built off the back end of the southern loading bays. "You fade left, I'll go long."

Mel was used to Rhe's odd allusions and strange phrases, and after seven years working together he knew what to do. Pulling his antenna down into his scalp to protect it if there were a fight, the Sassini slid through the crowd, his black-jacketed form fading into the crowd filling Market Street, before disappearing into a shadowed alley behind the stalls.

"I HATE THIS JOB," Rhe said out loud—the bad habit of having a partner, you talked to them even when they weren't there—as she strode forward through the crowd. And then, because Mel hated when she used hyperbole, she amended the thought. She didn't really hate the job. Just the shitty places they had to go to get it done.

Portside was a hellhole even among hellholes. Oh, it was clean, and safe enough. It had to be, to serve its purpose: take the lifters and transports in, unload, load, and send them back out again, for a price. It was an artificial world, built around the docks, and filled with transient workers and low-level techs, with a corrupt ream of Corporate skimming off the top.

The only people who came here without an exit ticket were the ones with no other choice. Or the poor bastards who were born here. Port owned them, used them, and left them to rot.

Teens, not wearing identifying jumpsuits, lounged with studied indifference against an empty stand, staring at her as she passed. The smoke from their dreamsticks rose over their heads, swirling purple and red in the air. She sneered, because it was expected, and muttered a hard "losers" as she passed, because otherwise they might think she was soft, a woman alone, an easy target.

They'd lost before they were born. No chance if you didn't have a lifeline, someone to get you off-planet, or into a career, and there were no careers here, if you didn't have a way in. Admin was HQ-level, port-workers were contract hire through vetted firms. Only jobs for the Port-born were day-hire muscle, street hustling, or whoring. No ways offplanet, just the same day in and day out, until dreamsticks and early death seemed like bright ideas.

It was sad, but it was also not her problem.

She followed Market Street, aware of the crowds around her, and the sense of Mel somewhere overhead, hoping that he had eyes on their unknown watcher, because she had no idea where he or she was.

The crowds were thinner at this end, the booths offering more expensive goods, some of them possibly even legal. She thought about stopping to look at one booth, the glitter of tanned parselskin catching her eye, but too aware of the skids in her bag that needed to be delivered, and how awkward it would be to have to explain them if the cops picked her up. Better to not go into any of the booths, anyway. She didn't want to lose her tail, after all. Not until they knew *why* they were being followed, anyway.

Taking a moment to look around, as though contemplating the offerings, she noted that the stall roofs were all connected, several meters overhead, with narrow walkways running along them, with a knee-high traverse perfect for resting a muzzle across. For all the Security tags they'd passed, there wasn't a single gold-code to be seen in the crowd, not even in plain suit. Presumably any Special Personages would be brought along secured roads, not these public passways. Otherwise she was going to resign and take up a new career as an assassin.

Their security was not her business right then, she reminded herself. Time was money, and she was wasting it.

Hoping to draw their watcher out of hiding, she slowed her pace, and tried to look distracted, an easy mark. "Here, watcher watcher watcher…"

She didn't expect to actually flush out anyone—that was Mel's job. She was just the bait.

JOSEY SHIFTED, uncomfortable. One of the targets he'd spotted had disappeared. If he blew this, or drew anyone's attention, Mather was going totally going to kill him, no way around it. He could feel the sweat tracking down his back, under the thin shirt Wane had given him last month, when she outgrew it. His toes clenched into the ledge he was sitting on, his buttocks tensing in agitation.

Dressed like that, with courier bags, they were supposed to have stayed in the Port proper, not gone wandering the Market. It would be easier to make a grab there, yeah, with the crowd, but the crowd also meant some might see him and blab, or worse, think there might be a reward and try to grab him.

But couriers had been too tempting a prize to pass up. If he could do that, Mather would be impressed, give him better locations to work, maybe even teach him a trade, make himself more useful.…

He checked the time—nearly curfew—and scanned the crowd frantically. The cricket was nowhere to be found, and he'd stupidly been counting on having the pairing to watch, but—there. The female was just heading up the stairs.

If he was fast, he could use the uplands, and get ahead of her, rather than being stuck behind. But he'd have to bolt.

"HELLO, HELLO, HELLO," Mel said. He had followed Rhe up the stairs, moving up the side of a store to the roof, and sliding along the plas tiles, keeping her in sight as best he could. He had gone down on all six legs, his face turned at a 90-degree angle. His species was as much at home on all six as two, but they had discovered that the other species reacted badly to their scuttling on the ground—some strange atavistic behavior that almost derailed interspecies relations before any treaties had been signed.

The smell of human sweat was particularly…disgusting. Rhelichi's skin was familiar, and with familiarity came a sort of comfort, but overall humans were the equivalent of old garbage for his species. And according to his olfactors, there was only one human up here with him, just ahead of his cluster-sister, who was giving an exceptionally excellent impersonation of a lost tourist.

It was possible that the human was not their watcher, but not probable. Not the way the watching-human was keeping pace with Rhe on the street below.

"What are you doing, watching-human? Who are you, and why am I wasting time chasing you down?"

Couriers were paid—and paid well—to not be noticed. They needed to know if this were simply a would-be mugger reaching out of his prey-pool, or the tendrils of something more.

Rhe adjusted the bag over her shoulder, pulling out a tablet as though to double-check a map. Ahead and above, the watcher-human tensed, arms resting on the railing as though preparing to leap.

It was a three-meter drop, and at least ten meters from where Mel was waiting. But Sassini were made for moving quickly.

Josey heard something skittle behind him, too many legs on plas, and panicked, scrambling backwards in an attempt to escape.

"Not so fast, human," he heard, even as a hard form crashed into him, knocking him over the railing, and to the ground, pulling the shiv out of his hand even as they hit.

Ah, shit. Please oh please don't let it be a Wastelander, he thought. Even Portside security would be better than that….

The smell of oranges and vanilla followed. Sassini. Shit. Shit shit shit. That was where the other half of the mark had gone. Mather was going to kill him, if they didn't. But either option was better than security sending him to a downside work camp….

"Hold still, human," the weight on his back told him, yanking his arms in a tight hold. He had never smelled a Sassini's breath before. It wasn't as nice as its body smell, sort of like stale coffee after it had been in the mouth for a week.

"Fuck you."

"Language." The alien sounded…amused? Josey went limp, considering that element as part of his brain tried to figure the odds of wriggling out from under and—

"What do we have here?" a new voice asked, coming from just above and ahead in the walkway. She definitely sounded amused. "Mel, let him up before you break the poor thing."

<hr>

THE SASSINI GOT him into an armlock, the exoskeleton weirdly, unexpectedly warm. He'd thought they'd be colder, somehow. But the human made up for it. She had found a chair in someone's stall, was leaning on it now, studying him like he was something new and not very interesting.

"You don't have the look of a professional—not a good one, anyway. Too scrawny, too underfed. So you're a grunt-level thief—maybe working for someone—who doesn't treat their people well, I'm guessing. Tell me who it is, and you walk away with only a few bruises."

"Not telling you anything."

They'd been over this a dozen times already, just different words. This time, though, the woman rolled her eyes, then sat down on the chair, resting her chin in her hands and staring at him like she was actually listening, this time. "All right. But why not?"

Josey stared at the woman like she'd just grown another nose. "Serious? Because I don't want to die?"

"Even if you don't tell us anything, your boss will assume that you did. Can't imagine they'll be too happy with you, then."

"Nope. They know I'm loyal."

Mather knew no such thing, and they were probably right about his reaction, but he wasn't going to admit that. Wasn't going to admit anything, not unless there was something significant in it or him, and there wouldn't be, because there never was.

It was almost past-curfew. The Market was starting to shut down. If they didn't let him go….

If he went back without having nipped anything, even if he didn't admit he'd been nipped himself....

There was no good way out of this. Not unless he pulled off the nip of his life.

He didn't let his gaze drift to the courier bags they'd stashed against the chair. They were within reach, almost as though they'd been put there to taunt him. If the Sassini didn't still have both arms in a lock behind his back, and by the way, that was starting to seriously ache.

"You want to make me think you're the good guys, you could let up on the snake-grip back there, maybe?

"Nope. Not until you give us something, first."

Josey had learned to stare from the best. He could do it all night, if he had to. If they kept him here until morning, and patrol didn't find them all. Assuming his arms didn't fall off, first.

<hr>

"This is going nowhere, and taking too long to do so."

Mal used his native tongue, making the kid flinch a little at the noise. Smart, though; no certainty a port rat like this hadn't picked up at least a little tradespeak. He looked to be smart enough, anyway; an eye to the chances but a pretty clear assessment of his options. She'd hoped that appealing to that would break him down a little, but no go.

Either he really believed his boss would reward loyalty, or he figured he was dead either way, and wanted to go out true.

Meanwhile, Mal was right: they were already late, and getting later. She rubbed her mouth with her hand, aware that it might look like indecision to anyone watching.

The kid didn't blink.

"All right, kid. Here's the playback. My partner is getting bored, and he thinks you smell bad, so he wants to cut your throat and dump you into the nearest 'cycler. Me, normally I humor him. But I hate waste, and I think killing you would be a waste. So how about we stop playing Tough at each other, and negotiate like adults?"

"Rhe, what are you doing?"

She ignored Mal. He'd catch up soon enough, and his growl added conviction to her lie about what he'd said.

"Already said I wasn't going to tell you who hired me."

"And I'm not going to ask again. But tell me this: what did they want?"

He was good—almost good enough. But there was the faintest flick of his eyes to the left.

Not the right, where the courier bags were stashed in clear sight, but the left. Her left hand, specifically.

"Oh ho." She leaned back, honestly surprised. She lifted her left hand, letting the black chip tacked to her hand glint under his gaze. "You don't want the skids—you want our ID! Mal, we've got ourselves a 'dent-runner!"

She was impressed, despite herself.

"That's a serious crime," her partner said, dropping back into First Common. "Maybe we should turn him in ourselves, pick up a bounty?"

"Too much paperwork, not enough cash," she said, shaking her head. "But I do see why he didn't want to talk. His boss—yeah, they'd assume he spilled his guts, they couldn't afford to do anything else. Maybe we should just kill him, do it fast as a mercy."

The boy's throat clenched, but his eyes never wavered from hers, his lip never trembled, and she decided, on the moment, that she kind of liked this kid. Tough, smart, a bit of a mouth, and if he thought he was good enough to lift a 'dent off skin without getting caught—and clearly, he did think that—he had some significant hand skills.

"Or," she said, watching the kid's face, "we could keep him."

Mal groaned, the kid's eyes went wide, and she grinned.

HE'D ASSUMED they'd kill him. At best, maybe toss him a coin if he spilled on Mather, and leave him to explain his way out of that. Instead, he was pore-damp from the 'fresher in an apartment in the Arcade—the Arcade!—staring at himself in a three-quarter mirror wondering who the hell thought grey looked good on anyone.

Grey for 'prentice. Grey for access to the docks. Grey for a way off Portside.

He fiddled with the neck tabs, frowning at his ears, suddenly startlingly visible without the mop of curls that had previously covered them. "Nobody's going to believe I'm any kind of spacer."

"Just don't throw up," the woman said. "Or pass out. Or talk. And you'll do fine."

Josey had a number of responses to that, but figured it wasn't smart to say a damn thing right now. The Sassini was leaning against the door, blocking his exit, and the human—Rheanna, she said her birth-name was, the other was Mal's clan-name for her—was standing behind him, her arms folded over her nearly non-existent chest as she studied his reflection critically.

"I looked worse when you found me," she said to the Sassini, who rolled his eyes. "You had just crashed your ship into the side of a mountain."

"Emergency landing, and I hadn't been the pilot, excuse you."

Josey almost thought he'd rather have them threatening him again.

"Are you sure you don't want to just abuse me and leave me on the side of the road for the bodybaggers to find?"

"You're nowhere near cute enough," Rhe said. "Plus, way too young. Come on. What've you got to lose? You think you had a future here, you want to stay so bad?"

Nobody wanted to stay Portside. Not even Mather. It was the principle of the thing, not....

And even without speaking it, everyone in the room knew that was the dumbest thing he'd ever thought.

With a put-upon sigh loud enough for the muckwucks in the topmost floor of the Arcade to hear, Josey opened the collar of the jumpsuit so it looked a little less idiotic, and walked toward the door, somewhat surprised when the Sassini moved out of his way.

Once through the doorway, he looked back over his shoulder. "Well? Are you coming, or not?"

If need drove, he could still steal their 'dents, and jump, next planetfall.

Euterpe's Song

MANNY FRISHBERG

1

First Light

Iná cupped her ear to hear the cave sing.

The winds blew endlessly but the cave only sang when it came from the right direction and blew so hard, no harder. Iná had heard many caves' songs—she recalled enough winters for the snow to stain her hair white, yet she still chewed her own meat.

The Able were on the Great Hunt; too old and too young left waiting, slept further in. Eldest, she watched. She listened. Hunger gnawed at her craw, a mouse gnawed on a boiled deer leg. She dove for the mouse but caught the shinbone instead.

Moonlight made shadows dance in the tooth marks. Iná imagined holes drilled between them. With a spear point she scratched a spot, then jammed it in with a rock and twisted, blew out the bone dust and did it again. The moon had gone and the sky faded by the time she had three round holes.

The wind picked up and the cave sang again. Old joints ached as she got up to present her gift to the singing wind. She walked to the cave's mouth and held her hand out, clutching the bone, aiming it into the face of the wind.

The bone sang.

She pulled it in and the cave's song returned. She tried again, twisting her hand around as she extended it. The bone caught the wind and sang out, but only when she held it some ways.

Iná went to sit close to the smoking embers and softly blew across the edge of the shinbone. It sang. She dropped it, then picked it up and tried it again. It sang a different tone. Iná looked down. Her hand covered two of the holes. She shifted her grasp and blew – another tone. She laughed. Then Iná tucked the bone into her breechcloth and went to sleep.

Passing into the Night World, Iná saw a giant, squatting on a mountaintop. She had Iná's bone, made giant too. As she blew over it and moved her hand, the bone sang one tone and another. Her fur lit afire in dazzling red-gold-yellow, like the sky lit afire by the sun's return. Light roiled as the bone-song continued. Iná shivered with delight at the bone's singing, at the giant's song, at the brilliant light washing over them. Then she awoke.

<hr>

When, at last, what food they had was eaten and the last of her great grandchildren licked clean, Iná walked out of the cave alone. It was dangerous, but her years were already too many to remember. She sat on an outcropping like the giant on her mountain and blew into her bone. Coaxing its song was harder for her than the giant. Her mouth was dry before she could make it sing every time.

In the Night World, Iná searched for three nights before she found the Flame Giant. This time she studied the giant's hands—her fingers danced, tapping out the giant's moves on her arm. Not even the display of light distracted her.

The next three days Iná stole away when the chance permitted and repeated the steps, making the bone sing the giant's song. Ächès and two more of the younger Ables had come back with strings of small animals for Iná and her daughters to prepare. So it took three days to teach the bone to sing the song all the way through. Playing it over and again, Iná could feel the sound bringing the worlds of day and night together.

Drowsy by the fire, she wondered what awaited her in the Night World. When she arrived, she felt no surprise to see the Flame Giant waiting for her. They played their bones together and the harmony filled Iná with the spirit of the Day. The flames spilled out of her eyes and nose and mouth and became the returning sun burning up the sky. The Flame Giant dove into the sun.

Iná understood. The Flame Giant had passed the sacred trust to her, to awaken the sun and call it home.

No one complained when Iná always took the late watch. Being old, she did not sleep so much but journeyed into the Night World when the sky was still light. Having a secret amused her. Secrets hardly existed in this world, though they abounded on the night side.

Alone on her rock before dawn, Iná would try other patterns with her fingers, teach the bone new songs, yet always, she remained faithful to the spirit within her and coaxed from the bone the tune that brought the sun home. She reveled in the sun's showiness through the warmer days but the returning cold settled into her own bones and her gait grew stiffer. She knew she had to share her secret, soon.

Iná thought about her daughters—certainly not sons—but she had outlived half her daughters already. A granddaughter, then. So she watched them more carefully, more thoughtfully than she had before. She admired Etnet's inquisitiveness and how good she was with her hands. Ntech, though, was implacable, a force to be reckoned with. Nothing would stop *her*.

When the moon was in hiding and the sky just beginning to fade, Iná carried Ntech outside and sat her on the rock. The girl awoke, frightened, but calmed by her grandmother's face. Iná produced the bone and began its song, calling the sun out from his night home. And again the next night, and the next again.

On the second day, Iná showed Ntech how she made the bone sing. The girl tried until the sun had put on his red evening coat. But the following day she made some noises and after a third, she could play the sun song, sort of.

In the Night World Iná saw the Flame Giant one more time.

Ntech sat on the rock and coaxed the tune to bring home the sun from the bone, filling her with the spirit of the flames.

2

Old Man With a Horn

"MAN, you should have heard that cat in his prime." The whispered voice carried across the length of the train station.

"Why? What happened to him?"

"Don't know," the voice echoed back. "One day he's on top, the next..." He snapped his fingers and let his head swing back and forth. "Smack, some say, but lots of hopheads play so sweet and sad."

It was the acoustics had led Ronnie to this spot, like standing in the middle of a monitor. He blew into the mouthpiece, fingers flashing up and down the keys, squeezing out the notes, his notes in staccato bursts. The man's leather soles scraped, and the woman's stiletto heels clacked on the concrete floor. He dropped a dollar into Ronnie's case and tugged at his lady's hand.

Ronnie matched the rhythm of their receding steps. Even he could hear the emptiness at the heart of the melody. He kissed the mouthpiece and played some more, breathing the despair past the bamboo reed, hearing the man's reproach echo in the notes.

Yeah. Blame it on the H, maybe in a way. Got caught in a sting, trying to cop quick between sets. Landed in the drunk tank—just for one night, but that had been all it took.

As a kid Ronnie was just okay. He switched from clarinet to tenor sax because it was shinier, made the high school marching band and caught the performing bug. Ronnie loved the attention, loved dressing in uniform and being somebody, out in front for once.

And then jazz had latched onto his soul. Funny thing, he'd been surrounded by it his whole life. Growing up, the old vinyl was always spinning—Bird and Ornette Coleman and Cannonball Adderly. But that was his father's music. Then, one night, seventeen and staying out so he wouldn't have to go home, he stumbled by an after-hours club, and this flute catches his ear. He goes in to see this old guy, white tufts coming out his ears, more wrinkles than face, and Ronnie can't turn away.

So he hangs out 'til the combo's packing up. As the old man passes Ronnie, he tips his head toward the door for the boy to follow. Then he opens the front door and stands half-in, half-out. And staring out into the night, he starts to blow. Behind him, Ronnie watches the sun peek over the Brooklyn piers.

It's a simple tune but Ronnie can't get it out of his head. He goes home and locates the notes on his sax, practicing until his fingers know their own way through. And as he plays, the song penetrates his heart; the horn becomes an extension of him. The song spills out unbidden, no layer of thought between his fingers and the keys.

He slept fitfully that night, awaking restless as the first, soft light showed on the horizon. Ronnie grabbed the saxophone case and raced to the roof of his building in his pajamas without knowing why. Sharp edged gravel stung his feet. The navy blue sky faded around the bottom edge. He took out the saxophone and twisted the mouthpiece into place. The song flowed through his body and out the horn, an aching beauty vibrated through him as the melody played him and the sun came up.

It had been like that every morning after.

With the spirit in him, he started getting gigs. Though he was underage, the club owners bent the rules—got him a counterfeit cabaret card for when the man from the Liquor Board came around. He got to learn from the masters when they came through town, absorbing everything he could. And every morning, he was out on his roof, playing that same old, simple song the same old way because, as he told the reporter from Downbeat, it was how the spirit moved him.

But fame and the muses are fickle, especially when you're young. Ronnie learned from the masters—learned to smoke reefer in the dressing room—learned how a little smoke could mellow you so the harmonies took on a soft, blue glow. He didn't drink much—his father drank all the time. But coke was another thing, a little pick-me-up until you took too much and you got all jittery. And when you overdid it, a little taste of heroin could smooth that rough edge out. Until, after a while the rough edges were always there, most acutely when he'd be warming up for a gig, but soon every night, and every day after a while, too.

Even before his arms were yanked back and he heard the handcuffs snap, Ronnie knew he was in trouble. Well past midnight, he was in Booking too late for Night Court. From the holding cell Ronnie could just see the window, high up in the concrete wall. His stomach roiled and a dull thudding pulsed behind his eyes. He heaved thin, bitter bile. The stale air smelled of old gym locker rooms, still but cold. The small patch of darkness faded—too slowly, as if time itself had lost the beat.

As he watched, Ronnie felt a tearing somewhere deep within him. As the morning light broke through the window, a hollowness consumed him, a void where something had resided inside him for so long he had forgotten it.

Another train roared into the station below his feet and Ronnie fingered his sax, readying himself for the crowd filing up the stairs past him. A few stragglers waited to listen as he started. Ronnie played them the flutist's simple, haunting melody. The emptiness reverberated from the tiles, along with the clink of someone dropping a few coins into his case, and fading footsteps echoing through the station.

3

Last Call

HIS NOSE PRESSED against the window, Abe waved good-bye, just like when he was a child setting off on a road trip with his parents. The automated launch sequencer counted down the final seconds for the last ark leaving the Earth.

He had prepared for this day for over a year. Abe bought birds—magpies, mynahs, mockingbirds and macaws, parakeets and parrots, as many as he could find and afford to feed. Each morning, when he came home at dawn, he would play them his tune, a simple string of flute notes, repeated relentlessly, all day long, for as many days as it took.

He had always been Abe, never Abraham. His hair had gone from black to nearly pure white, to black again thanks to his vanity, in the twenty-four years since the spirit filled him and the song had entered his life. Still, he never tired of playing it, never wished he did not have to play it, seeing the sun rise as he did.

He loved the dawn, always. Even when clouds obscured the fiery colors, he basked in the changing tones of pearlescent grays. Not even a downpour could chase him away.

He had prepared for leaving by taking long walks through the urban forest and the dwindling preserves of grassland and trees; Abe went to capture the colors of the new solar spectrum, brighter, the scientists said, than in ancient times, to collect them in his camera, in his memories.

"Memories are a fickle thing," he told his birds one day, when he was certain they had learned to sing, and that a few words would not interfere with his plan. "I think I can recall a time when I did watch the sun rise, but maybe I only remember recalling it. I want to think I will remember all the colors under the sun. My sun." At times like that he considered staying.

If he did, he would not be alone. The robots would remain, as would those too frail or sick or stuck in their ways to make the leap. But he would not last long here, as they would not, so it only postponed things a little.

Some of the birds had been slow to learn. Some never mastered the rhythm, or the tones came out wrong. Over time, enough did, though. And he could see a spark in some of their eyes, curiosity and more, a hint at deeper understandings. He could only hope it could be enough. He could only wish that it was.

He'd brought nesting materials home because that, too, was part of the plan. He had learned all he could about their mating habits and set up spaces where the most attentive birds had the best chance. His efforts bore fruit but by then so much time had passed he would never know if the offspring would learn their new song for themselves.

He clamped his helmet on and adjusted the airflow. Abe regretted not being able to see the sun one last time, but he still had to get to his pod before liftoff. The other passengers had all stowed themselves for the Long Sleep already. He laid back in his pod as the first-stage engines roared to life. He had to fight the increasing gravity to lift the hose connectors and push them into his suit, then hit the button to seal the pod and initiate sedation before chilling his body. With his last act of will in this solar system, Abe turned his head to take a last look at the sky through the slim strip of window he could see.

He breathed in the sweet-pungent scent of nitrous oxide being mixed into his air supply and felt himself diving into the depths of his mind, felling less and less of the crushing pressure of rising through the atmosphere, awareness fading into an indigo cloud.

His eyes popped open—the narrow edge of the sky had become dark as night, the sun behind them. A deep pain pressed outward on his chest and he wondered if this was what a heart attack felt like. Then the pressure faded, leaving Abe feeling exhausted and emptied. He drew the anesthetic gas deep into his lungs again.

Falling into the cloud, he imagined a mynah, perched on the windowsill of his apartment, faithfully mimicking his flute as the sun showed its first rays on the edge of the horizon.

Child of Two Worlds

S. B. SEBRICK

"Why did I let you talk me into this?" Isabell muttered from the shadows.

"Shhh," Deegan hissed, pulling her into the corner of the alley.

Torches flickered in the street. Dozens of steel and leather-clad men hurried past, heading to the East Gate.

"I doubt the Goddess of Familial Love would agree with what we are about to do," he said. "This is the only way to make them understand me. We may even save the city."

A heavy boom rumbled in the distance, rattling a couple of nearby windows, as if to emphasize his point. The Talarian Horde hammered against the city's doorsteps, fighting the church's protective spells on the gate with the magic of their own violent deity.

"Save the city? Of course. Assuming the townsfolk don't kill us first. Or afterward, for that matter," Isabell shot back. "Why can't we just sneak onto the battlefield and let you do your thing there?"

"Too risky," Deegan said. "One stray arrow and I'd be killed."

"Not like raising an army of corpses from the local church's graveyard," Isabell sighed, rolling her eyes. "That's completely safe. No chance the priest might take notice and burn us to death where we stand."

"This is a battle, Izie. Everyone's focused on *avoiding* a one-way trip to the graveyard. Not visiting one. The civilians are huddled away in the inner keep and the soldiers are watching the walls for more attacks. No one is watching the dead."

"Fine," Isabell replied. "But if we are caught, I'm insisting you brought me out here by force."

"I wouldn't have it any other way," Deegan said. He took her hand, fighting a nervous quelling sensation in his stomach. "You will survive this, even if I have to carry you out of the city myself."

Isabell blinked in surprise. "Deeg…we're going to get through this."

"Let's go."

At the alley's edge, Deegan carefully watched the corners of the intersecting streets. Years spent picking pockets and dodging guards gave him a firm sense of the soldier's movements. He led Isabell down narrow side streets. They passed an apothecary, windows shattered, door broken in. Looters flitted around the shop. Even the criminal element knew the city was in real peril. The looters would head west after this, to slip out through exits of their own devising. Deegan clenched his fists, drawing a squeak of pain from Isabell.

"Sorry," he muttered, moving her hand to his shoulder. "Better to hang onto me, in case I need to use my hands for spell casting." He glanced over his shoulder at the apothecary. Thieves needed the city as much as the honest man. What good would retreat provide? If the region fell to the Horde, where would the thieves go then? Better to stand and fight.

Turning back to the cobblestone road, Deegan swallowed his anger. If it weren't for his Dualist magic, he'd be running as well. He set his sights on the nearby cathedral's bell tower.

Torches ahead.

Deegan jerked to the left, scrambling down a side alley. The soldiers wouldn't kill them on sight, but there wasn't time to argue the merits of his plan.

"Who goes there?" someone cried. "Reveal yourself!"

Deegan glanced over his shoulder and winced. Of course, he'd gotten clear in time, but they'd seen Isabell's cloak as she followed after him.

She paled, glancing at the road. "What do we—"

Deegan dragged her down the alley. Heavy boots smacked against cobblestones as the soldiers advanced, though they still hadn't rounded the corner yet.

The end of the alley, a side entrance to the graveyard, was blocked off by a tall wrought-iron gate. Headstones peeked out from among bushes and shrubs on the other side of the barrier, as if teasing him. A large rusty padlock kept the gate sealed, heavily corroded by time. No skill with lock picks could undo that obstacle.

Deegan slammed his fist against the gate, reviewing his options. None of them were...subtle.

"You there!" four men cried, hurrying toward Deegan and Isabell. "No civilians allowed in the outer district. Can't you see what's going on? We're at war!"

"We are here for—" Isabell said, but Deegan pushed her aside.

"No time," he insisted. Raising both hands, the left toward the gate and the right toward the soldiers, he looked inward. After half-a-day spent in meditation, power stewed inside him, spells awaiting release.

A shockwave ripped out of his left hand, punching through the iron gate. To his right, the soldiers were subjected to the backdraft, the spell's opposite effect. It jerked them forward, their torches clattering aside. They spun and rolled toward Deegan as his spell pushed the gate's remains away from his position.

"Hurry!" Deegan said.

Isabel scrambled ahead of him, tripping over a twisted chunk of iron. She rolled onto her back, staring pale-faced at the nearby guards, but she was clear of the fence.

"Good enough," Deegan said, hoping over the twisted iron remains. Again, he extended his hands.

The soldiers scrambled to their feet, drawing their weapons.

"Torches!" one cried, peering into the darkness. "Does anyone still have—"

That was all the time Deegan needed. The earth in front of him heaved. A tall slab of stone rose to replace the broken iron gate. Behind him, the earth gave way, the spell's backdraft revealing a hole behind Deegan of the same size as the earthen wall.

"Deegan, I know it's you!" one of the men shouted. "They warned us you might try something foolish. The King will see you hung for this!"

"We don't have much time," Deegan said grimly.

"You've got that right," Isabell hurried to her feet. She limped on her left ankle, but swatted his concerned hand away. "What's next?"

"I need to reach the center of the graveyard," Deegan said. "There isn't time for subtlety now."

"Are you sure you can get the dead outside the city?" Isabell asked, matching his pace. They cut to the left, pushing through a nasty rosebush.

"The irrigation grate, beneath the northern wall," Deegan said, his mouth dry as he eyed the shadowy gravestones. His heart raced and his palms felt moist. He could feel the bodies stretching out before him, empty vessels waiting for someone to fill them. "The church's enchantments on the city walls prevent Dualists from breaking into the city, not out."

"That's right at the base of the cathedral," Isabell said uneasily, pointing northward. "What if a priest notices? I don't want to be caught between two Dualists. Or behind them either. Cursed backdraft."

The imposing stone structure, so beautiful in the light of the day, looked more like a stone-skinned many-eyed monster at night. Candles within attested to the efforts of the church's priests, laboring to fuel the powers of their brethren on the front lines.

"They won't bother to look outside, unless a nearby patrol sounds the alarm." Deegan prayed he was right. He hadn't worked for the church in years, but they were heavily steeped in tradition. Surely their protocols hadn't changed so drastically in a single decade.

Deegan and Isabell reached the highest point of the graveyard. The distant rumbles of war seemed far away now, a minor inconvenience next to the might of the Gods. The dark hid most of the Cathedral's beauty, but added a sense of immense power.

Deegan's plan would make any priest cross indeed. He turned, facing the dead. Hundreds of marble stones winked back at him, marking the remains of so many departed loved ones. The richest and most powerful people the city had ever known. He reached out tentatively at first, like a child taking his first step into a bakery full to the brim of every manner of sweets.

"W—wait," Isabell sputtered, gripping his shoulder. "*These* are the ones you're going to raise?"

"Yes." Deegan furrowed his brow as he looked into her eyes. "That's always been the plan."

"You can't raise the people the city *remembers*," Isabell said. Her soft hair tickled his face and smelled like strawberries. "How would you feel if someone dug your parents up from the grave?"

"I was raised in a cave by a band of corpses, Izie." Deegan shrugged. "Corpses are…comforting. Honest. Obedient. No hidden agendas or lies."

"If you raise the city's loved ones, they will hang you for turning their loved ones into killers," Isabell insisted, stomping her foot.

"Then how do you suggest I do this?" Deegan grumbled, his nostrils flaring angrily. Another hollow boom rumbled through the city. "We need an army. Right now. Did you come along to help me or to stop me?"

"Look beyond the gravestones," Isabell said, touching his arm.

Deegan paused. He looked down the hill. The gravestones got progressively smaller and less ornate, as only the church's most respected and wealthy patrons could afford a plot so close to the cathedral.

There, at the base of the hill, hundreds of stakes lined the southern edge of the graveyard. Centuries of unnamed bodies collected from the street or the headsman's axe.

"Can you manage this battle with only the nameless dead at your command?" she asked.

"I hope so," Deegan sighed, giving her hand a grateful squeeze "You are right, Izie. I couldn't do this without you."

When he let her go, her face paled, looking over his shoulder. "Deeg?"

Deegan turned. A dozen yellow torches flickered in the distance, gathering like a swarm of fireflies and converging on the graveyard.

"Let's go," Deegan said.

She refused, jerking him to a halt. "I can slow them down." She squeezed his hand, looking deep into his eyes. "You will need time to raise so many and get them out of the city."

"I know," Deegan sighed, shaking his head. "I don't know the living well enough, though. How can I keep them from hating me?"

"Pretend they are me," Isabell said. There was a raw tension to her voice, a desperate sincerity. "Treat them like you would me. Now *go*."

Swallowing his fear, Deegan plunged deeper into the graveyard. Part of him longed to raise the rich dead around him, ensure Isabell's safety by force of numbers and somehow *make* the people see the truth. The dead were tools, no more. They weren't monsters or dangerous in the hands of the right master.

How to make the people understand?

The gravestones grew progressively smaller and less pronounced as Deegan rushed down the hill. His mouth felt dry and his heart hammered in his chest. Isabell was his interpreter when it came to the things of the world.

What if, in order to win the battle, he did something the people couldn't forgive? What if, in saving the town, they tried to execute him for aiding them in all the wrong ways? Or Isabell? Would the guards arrest her on the spot and converge on him? No, he had to trust she could talk her way out of this. She had to.

"Treat them like I would Izie," Deegan grumbled. "Trust a diplomat's daughter to hide the means of saving the city in a riddle." He stumbled over a squat tombstone. The cool grass leapt up to meet him and he regained his balance in the midst of a field of short stakes. He could feel the dead lying in wait underground, marked by a garden of blank stakes. Silent. Empty.

Ready.

Casting aside his concerns, Deegan closed his eyes and reached into the earth with his Dualist powers. Separating the unnamed graves from the rich was surprisingly easy. They could afford to keep their plots an equal distance apart from the rest. Here, the bodies were stored in tangled heaps.

"Come on, come on, come on," Deegan whispered. "I need you. The city needs you. Your city needs you."

Energy trickled through his chest and down his arms, an itching, burning sensation. From his hands, black vapor poured onto the ground. The gas seeped into the ground, driven by Deegan's conscious will.

This was the magic the church feared. A kind without backdraft. Powers that pierced death itself, after a fashion.

The first body quivered in response. Deegan gasped, "Yes, yes!"

Then ten. Twenty. But not enough to face the Horde beyond the walls. The tingling in his arms intensified, as if an ant swarm were coating his limbs. Crawling. Gnawing. Feasting. He poured more black vapor into the earth. Fifty. A hundred now. More. The tingling shifted into pain, then trembling. Deegan fell to his knees, hands resting on the soft grass.

Black cracks cut down his arms in a spider-web formation, like mud after baking in the summer heat for too long. Warm blood oozed down his arms, leaving the patch of grass beneath him slick with crimson. Deegan fell onto his side. The world blackened for a precarious moment.

A foul odor rushed over him as the earth gave way to hungry groans. Foul, but so familiar. He sighed and smiled contently. Comforting even.

They stood around him expectantly. Faces blank and open. Toothy maws hanging agape. Their bodies were suspended in various stages of decay. Some more bone than flesh. They wore tattered leather or linen, burial clothes partially eaten by worms and time. Their fingers ended in sharp claws. Despite their feeble appearance, Deegan could feel an otherworldly strength flowing through them.

"You're here." Deegan laughed with glee. They watched him, motionless, his words sparking not a single emotion. So gloriously simple. "You're finally here! It's been so long. I've missed your kind so much."

Yellow light touched the corpses. Men shouted from the top of the hill. A horn rang out in alarm. The tones of the cry set Deegan's teeth on edge. They were already marking his creations as enemies of all living. Deegan spat on the ground.

"You will prove them wrong," Deegan tried to rise. His legs spasmed and he flopped back onto the earth, smashing his fist in frustration against the slick grass, red with his blood.

The soldiers' cries were louder now. There was no more time.

"Carry me," Deegan said to the closest corpse, a sturdy creature with no neck and surprisingly thick muscles. The creature obeyed, holding Deegan like an infant

"I will call you Base," Deegan said. "The rest of you are my Arms.

Now, all of you, head west. Follow the irrigation ditch. Take me to the city wall."

The undead army moved with surprising swiftness. A few arrows hissed at their back, marking the soldiers' advance. The projectiles stuck uselessly in a couple of his minions' arms and legs. One frail corpse, a woman with long hair and twisted bones, took an arrow in the skull and collapsed.

"Morons," Deegan grunted. "If I was a threat I'd be attacking them, not running away." He glanced at the irrigation ditch, eight feet wide and nearly as deep. Another arrow sailed past, close enough to for Deegan to hear the *hiss* of approach and the *thunk* of wood against bone.

"Into the ditch. Run. We will have to punch through the grate together."

Deegan's forces moved into the ditch, a tightly packed band of living corpses, nearly two hundred strong. The pursuing arrows faded as Deegan's undead outdistanced the soldiers.

"Hold me over your shoulder," Deegan said to Base. "In case I have to protect us with magic."

The ride was a lot less comfortable as Base's thick shoulder jabbed into Deegan's chest with each step. They were at the outer limits of the city. The buildings were smaller and more rundown. A single civilian or two, too stubborn to abandon their homes, took one look at Deegan's rotting forces and bolted into the darkness, screaming. Perhaps the nearby patrols would find him easily after all.

Base lurched to a halt so quickly that Deegan fell backwards into the muck.

"Slow down gradually next time," Deegan scolded, rising to his feet. Base grunted, a blank and hollow sound. "These people have a hard enough time trusting me when I smell like sweat and old books. Ugh."

Base did not reply, staring ahead with the empty expression Deegan once found so comforting.

"Head's as empty as the marketplace after a plague," Deegan sighed, shaking his head. He pivoted, facing the rest of his forces. "Now, why did the rest of you stop?"

The rest of the undead, his Left and Right Arms, had indeed hit the irrigation grate as one. They'd run into the thing in mass.

"No, no, no," Deegan shouted, stomping his foot. "Back up. You need to tear it down. Not with your teeth, Left Arm! Does that iron look edible to you?"

Both Arms clawed at the iron grate in turn, but the metal was Dualism reinforced and anchored in the bottom of the city wall. A heavy rumble echoed through the city, coming from the east, where light and fire flashed. Even at this distance, Deegan could make out the screams. He ran his fingers through his hair, trying to order his thoughts.

"Fine then. Arms, step back."

The undead obeyed.

Extending his left hand toward the target and his right hand behind him, Deegan sent a blast of force into the iron grate. The barrier blew apart, torn chunks of iron shooting down and away from him. Despite the need for secrecy, Deegan let out a squeal of delight. As he'd theorized, the wall was much better protected against magical attacks from *outside.*

"Arms, get moving," Deegan ordered, swaying on the edge of the ditch, fatigue gradually claiming the use of his limbs. "Base, catch me."

The burly corpse reached out and managed to save Deegan from falling into the mire.

"Move *through* the opening," Deegan shouted. "Gather beneath cover on the other side and prepare for battle."

"Who goes down there?" a soldier called from atop the wall. "What was that awful noise? Are you a Dualist?"

"Yes, I am Deegan of Coldwell! I am here to save the city. Whatever you do, don't shoot us!"

"The Horde is all the way over there, young one," the soldier shouted back. "What do you plan to do from down there?"

"Well you just sit up there and find out what I'm doing," Deegan said. "Arms, Base, march *through* that godforsaken hole!"

<hr>

THEY GATHERED in a copse a short walk from the wall, well out of arrow shot. Deegan shakily rested his weight on a makeshift crutch he'd fashioned from a broken tree branch. A heavy silence lay over the trees.

"The Horde are the ones wearing *animal fur*," Deegan said. After the debacle at the gate, he wasn't taking any chances. "Not metal! If it's wearing metal, keep your distance. I don't want any misunderstandings."

They watched him with blank expressions.

"So, if they are wearing animal fur, you must kill them. Take them apart," Deegan said. "Don't eat them. Take and use their weapons only if you are skilled with them, and move on to the next target. Got it?"

A chorus of hollow grunts echoed through the copse of trees.

Another flash of light from the east. Something in the distance, impossibly heavy, thundered to the earth.

"March to the Eastern Gate and go to work. Remember, if it's a human wearing fur, kill them!"

The undead groaned in agreement, marching toward the flashes of light and screams of the dying. Deegan wobbled unsteadily, Base appearing at his side just in time, scooping Deegan up into the thickly muscled corpse's arm.

They moved through the underbrush with surprising speed.

A Horde scout burst from the foliage, firing his bow into the crowd. He tried to sprint away, but Deegan's forces were too swift. The scout went down, torn apart by sharp claws and even sharper teeth. Deegan shuttered against the sound. Perhaps the people were right to be afraid.

A couple more Horde scouts popped up. The undead clamored over them in a swarm, reducing their targets to patches of crimson goo in moments. Yes, surely this would be enough power with which to save the city. Better yet, with their lookouts killed, the Horde wouldn't see Deegan's forces coming.

They crested a rise in the terrain, overlooking the carnage. The mighty East Gate, once blessed with the Gods' own magic, lay in a broken heap. Through the opening Deegan saw a thin line of steel-clad soldiers standing against a mob of Horde forces.

The real trouble was the Dualists. A thin line of spell casters stood behind each force, the church's priests pitting their knowledge and faith against the Horde's shamans. Because of the backdraft, the terrain behind each of the casters was constantly exploding or freezing or erupting with divine power. The hands of the Gods extended through their acolytes, ripping into the physical world.

Deegan's troops advanced straight for the shamans, right toward their backdraft.

"No, no, no!" Deegan cried, pointing at the terrain behind the Horde's shamans. "You wouldn't last three breaths in there. Left Arm, circle to the left. Right Arm, circle to the right. On my mark, flank them!"

The undead shuffled off, following Deegan's bidding. Deegan extended his hand. The air in a one-foot circle before him rippled, amplifying his vision as if he were standing a dozen feet from the wall. The details of the battlefield emerged on the swirling air.

The Horde had used roughly constructed siege towers set on wheels to protect their troops from the archers atop the city wall. Horde bodies littered the base of the wall, blood-coated stones and patches of steaming oil marking the city's other defenses. The massive battering ram lay abandoned on the side of the road leading up to the east gate.

As his forces marched, he felt his connection to them weaken. Deegan gasped at the sensation. That was a weakness the textbooks never mentioned!

"Take me closer," Deegan said to Base, pointing to a cluster of trees on the right side. "But stay behind cover. I need to be close enough to feel them."

By the time the Left and Right Arms were in position, so was Deegan. His timing was none too soon. One of the shamans landed a ball of fire, engulfing a half-dozen soldiers. The priests rushed to magically douse the flames, but the Horde fighters were already there, forcing their way into the city.

Attack, Deegan thought, aiming all of his rage at the shamans ahead of him.

The undead charged from the left and right, letting forth a primal roar, the unearthly magic permeating their very beings, all directed through him at the shamans.

Deegan closed his eyes, tapping into his connection with the corpses. The visions of both his Left and Right Arms flashed before him. The shamans shrieked in fear, turning and striking out at Deegan's forces with heat or cold.

The attacks snuffed away dozens of Deegan's minions. However, each spell's backdraft hit several of the Horde's own shamans. The Horde's fighters pulled away from the battle line, falling back to support their shamans. With each blow of a Horde fighter, an undead connection vanished.

A painful buzzing built up in his mind as he managed dozens of bodies at once, trying to coordinate all of their attacks. Sparse archer fire rained down from the wall, but Deegan couldn't tell if they were trying to help him against the Horde. Through flickers in the chaos, Deegan noticed the city soldiers reforming.

He flinched as he felt one fighter pull a corpse's head clean off. He was losing. How could he turn the tide?

Withdrawing his focus back to his own body, Deegan forced himself to see the entire battlefield. The city's best soldiers stood resolutely within the broken city gates, their faces pale with fear. They were so few now.

The memory of Isabell's face as she turned to face the soldiers in the courtyard cleared his mind. The bloodlust faded. The longing for power. The thirst for complete control of his surroundings.

"Treat them like I would treat Isabell," Deegan muttered. "How can I show them? How can I allay their fears? Base. Take me close enough to reach the walls with my mind."

The smell of burned flesh grew thick around them, broken shamans lying upon the ground. The skulls on their staffs were clearly human. Through the chaos Deegan saw a flash or two of heat. A couple of shamans had survived and organized a real resistance.

"Base. Put me down." Base obeyed.

Deegan knelt and put his hands to the earth.

"More," he said, reaching out with his senses. He hissed in pain as the wounds on his arms opened up again. Warm blood oozed down his forearms. The world tilted dizzily. "We need more."

He reached out to the fallen bodies he once controlled, but they were too battered to re-use. The Horde's dead, however, were another story.

Gritting his teeth, he focused his efforts on the Horde's fallen, lining the outside of the walls. The dark vapor traveled beneath the earth, only rising up to fill the lungs of the *Horde's* dead. The tall, mighty warriors drew breath anew, rising from the earth like silent wraiths. Even from this distance, Deegan's mouth hung ajar as he felt the difference.

"Fresh corpses are so much stronger." Shaking himself from the realization, he took control and aimed them at the throng of the living Horde troops.

Kill them, he ordered.

If the city folk's dead were strong, these ones were mighty. They dove into the circle of foes with reckless abandon, biting, breaking and tearing their way into the enemy ranks.

Finally, the last shaman shrieked out a curse, and the battlefield erupted in a small quake. The force hurled Deegan's troops thirty feet into the air. The collision with the earth would have killed most men, but his undeads' limp bodies endured. They rose to their feet. Blank faces awaiting new orders.

Deegan collapsed onto his side. The cracks along his arms re-opened, oozing crimson streaked with black. His head throbbed with pain as he forced himself to rise to his feet. Retrieving a broken spear, he held himself upright, facing the soldiers and priests still lining the gate. They faced the undead, eyes wide, faces pale, tightly gripping their weapons.

All of you, form a circle, Deegan commanded, hobbling toward the front lines. If he wanted to prove to Isabell that he wasn't a threat, how would he do it?

The massive lumbering corpses formed a ring, each standing within arm's length of the other. They hefted their heavy maces in both hands, ready to strike. Deegan made sure the remaining corpses from the city graveyard did the same.

Soldiers at the gates and along the walls shifted their weight nervously from one foot to the other. A couple archers loosed arrows, which sunk into undead shoulders and legs without effect.

Once they were all in position, Deegan grit his teeth. He could take this undead force and walk away. Build an army so powerful the world of men could not threaten him. Or he could park this force outside the city and swear them to the King's service. Put the rest of the King's military to shame. Show the church the folly of their ways.

Despite the carnage around him, he remembered the strawberry scent of Isabell's hair, her light-hearted laugh. There was so much more to being human than having raw power. So much more to the life he wanted than these blank-faced servants. The people had to see his sincerity, his gentleness.

Nodding to himself, he prayed Isabell was right and that he'd understood her meaning. He gave the final order.

Decapitate the corpse on your right.

As one, the undead attacked with all their might. The undead bodies collapsed to the earth.

Deegan walked into clear view, hobbling along. A long shadow stretched from his feet to the city gate, the sun peeking up behind him. The battle had gone on much longer than he'd realized. Perhaps the sun would make him look more imposing, and the people would overlook the feces and urine stains on his tunic. And the blood. And the odd black-edge scars lining his arms.

"Does the City of Dawnshire have room for a battered Dualist?" Deegan called. He paused, clutching his makeshift walking stick. "Or is saving the city not work a bath, fresh clothes and a loaf of bread?"

"Let him pass," a gruff voice cried from the rear of the battle line.

Soldiers stood aside. Isabell stood next to General Tallwin, an unshaven man in his mid-forties, wearing blood-spattered chainmail.

Behind them, the priests watched Deegan intently. Their eyes were unblinking, their features stiff in anger or fear. They weren't howling for his execution. But was their silence a sign of forgiveness for raising the dead, or fear of the general's wrath?

Isabell hurried to his side. "Are you all right?" she asked, pulling a roll of bandages from her belt "Who did this to you?"

"Me," Deegan replied.

Isabell bound the cracks in his flesh. The throbbing pain brought the world back into focus. They approached the broken city gates.

When he reached the General, Deegan paused, eyeing the man. The General's mace hung from his belt, dripping with fresh blood. Smoldering holes in his chainmail attested to his willingness to face the enemy head on, in the defense of his city. His boots however, were stained with the familiar stench of feces.

"You were watching the whole time, ready to kill me," Deegan said aloud, though given the massive fatigue weighing on him, he couldn't summon the ire he should have felt.

"If you turned on the people," The General said. "Instead, you saved them. I can't speak for the rest of Dawnshire, but from the bottom of my heart, well done."

"Thank you," Deegan said.

The soldiers visibly relaxed, though the priests whispered back and forth to each other.

Deegan took a deep breath and tried to huff in pride, only to cough and lean heavily on Isabell.

"Easy," she said, holding him upright. "Just a little while longer. Then you can rest."

"We will see you tended to," the General said. "On behalf of Dawnshire, I thank you, Deegan of Coldwell, for saving our fair city."

"You're welcome, sir," Deegan said.

"You have great potential," the General said. "The city will remember this for generations to come. It's not every day our own dead rise up to save us."

"In some ways, I feel like the dead always do," Deegan said, glancing over his shoulder at the army he'd just cast aside. "Their stories give us something to live by. To strive and fight for."

"What do you fight for?" The General asked. "If you were after power, you could have kept that army you just destroyed. Greed or fame, as well."

"I'm a child of two worlds," Deegan said, shrugging. "The living and the dead's. But the dead's rest would be hollow indeed, without the spark of life to give it meaning."

Leaning on Isabell's shoulder, he gave her hand a loving squeeze and added, "I just want to protect our worlds. My world."

Run, Lagomorph

G. DAVID NORDLEY

THE CREEK GURGLED with white water and white noise. Orion winked through the pine trees while Leo, with Mars, shone brilliantly from just over the treetops. John Williams conducted memories through my ear buds, and my second Black Butte Porter was almost gone. A three-beer night? I'd done twenty pages today and felt uncommonly good, and the ears on the glowing rabbit by the picnic table seemed to twitch in approval. I lifted my mug to my lips and finished the draught.

Yeah, it took about that long for the glowing bunny's presence **to** sink into my critical awareness.

I shut my eyes as Wallace and Washington's "Pink Elephants on Parade" began to crowd the "Imperial March" out of my head. I shook my head, opened my eyes and the glowing rabbit was still there. Experimentally, I shut one eye, then the other. Still there. I paused the "Imperial March." Still there. Most definitely not a pachyderm. Wallace and Washington began to fade from my mind, as I contemplated the glowing rabbit.

On the slopes of Mount Hood, I was a fair distance from the Hanford nuclear reservation where such things were rumored to exist, courtesy of World War II and cold war expediency combined with ignorance and budget problems. Well, rabbits run. Maybe a rabbit, I thought, raised on a diet of grass grown in tritium-contaminated water, then painted with a phosphor encapsulated in nanobeads....

"Mr. Miller, will you help me?" the rabbit asked in a high pitched and raspy whisper that was just barely audible. "Pink Elephants" made a second appearance in my head, to be banished by a vigorous headshake.

"Sorry to bother you," the rabbit said.

"No, no," I said before it could jump away. "I'm just trying to clear my head. This is very, ah, unexpected."

"I can understand that."

"How did you know my name?"

"It's on the reservation sign at the front of your campsite."

"Of course. You can read."

"One has plenty of spare time in a cage lined with newspaper in a lab with closed captioned television shows."

"Uh, do you have a name?"

"Yes, but since I'm being sought, I'd rather not burden you with it. I'm a Lepus townsendi, obviously GM. I guess you can call me Jack."

"Jack Rabbit," I said.

"Well, Jack Hare would be more precise, but we have more pressing matters. Is it possible to go some place where I am less visible?"

"In the tent. I'll turn the light on." I was going to need that third Black Butte anyway, I thought.

At age 53, to save my back, I'd gotten myself a tent I could stand up in. I grabbed another Porter out of the cooler, plopped down on the steel folding chair—the back again—and waved my arm around. "Make yourself at home."

Jack settled in off my left side, where he could see both me and the entrance.

I was forgetting my manners. "Do you want some beer?"

"That would be an interesting experiment for some other time. We're about to have company." Jack hopped under my cot, hidden by a towel hanging over the edge.

Huh? "Jack?"

A confused minute later, I heard voices outside the tent.

"Miller? Ed Miller," someone with a gruff basso voice inquired.

I got up, pushed the flap aside, exited to find two six-foot-plus men, one heavy, one rangy, suited in camou with rifles. I zipped the screen flap back in place. "Bugs," I explained. "What can I do for you?"

"This is going to seem a bit strange."

"Try me. I'm a science fiction writer."

"There's a mutant rabbit on the loose. It glows kind of a lime green if it's really dark. We need to bring it back."

I nodded to the rifles. "Safe?"

"Uh," They looked at each other.

I patted my right crew pants pocket as if there were something other than a cell phone in it.

"Okay," Heavy said. Rangy shrugged and satisfying clicks ensued. That would give Jack maybe another second if he bolted—might be enough.

"I don't know of any mutation that would make a rabbit glow."

"That's what they..." Heavy started before Rangy jabbed him with an elbow. Too late.

"Who's "they?" I asked.

"Nobody. We're just hunting rabbits."

"Glowing rabbits?"

"From Hanford. All sorts of weird stuff up there."

"Why?"

"Damn it, have you seen a glowing rabbit or not?"

I raised my Porter bottle. "Working on it."

"Look," Rangy said. "It's not funny. Radiation. Isotopes. Mutations. Can't have that stuff running around loose. We can't say who we're working for and they didn't tell us much. Classified, understand? Now, if you say anything we'll have to shoot you...."

I started to reach for my cell phone....

"Or have you picked up or something," Heavy added, quickly.

"My guess, gentlemen, and it's just a guess, is that the authorities would be much more interested in you than me. I'm retired Air Force and still have some connections. Now..." I summoned a command voice I hadn't used since Officer's Training School, "*Just what is going on here?*"

They actually backed up two steps. Heavy's mouth was a line, his eyes wide and looking from side to side. He might be anticipating action nobody else should see.

Rangy sighed. "We work part time for a guy who has a contract with Halfast Biotech Science who have leased buildings on Hanford. I told him that we'd run into people who wouldn't buy the B.S. cover story, I just didn't think it would be the first one. We'll likely be let go if you blab about this..." He sighed. "...but I have to start somewhere. Something got out that hops and glows in the dark. I dunno what makes it glow in the dark. Maybe not radiation, because we didn't get any radiation hazard briefing, equipment, or anything. But they really want it back."

"Dead or alive?" I asked.

"We aren't really equipped for 'alive,'" Heavy growled.

"Yeah, I can see that. You have a card with a phone number?"

Rangy shrugged, reached in his pocket, and showed me a card. "It's some doctor at the lab we're supposed to notify. Can you take a picture? It's the only card I have."

I did, and sent them off into the woods.

Once I was inside the tent with the flap zipped closed, Jack nosed slowly out from under the cot, quivering like it was already down to the thirties.

"Th...th...th...thank you."

"You heard everything?"

He twitched his ears. "They're much better than yours."

"Were you intentional or a mistake?"

"Both. It's complicated; I don't know the whole history, but what I do know would take hours to relate. Some of my litter mates share some of my traits, but not all. We're all supposed to be sterile. But they aren't taking chances."

"Do they know you can talk?"

"Only one, Dr. Janet Jones, and she disappeared. That's one reason I escaped. I wanted to vanish on my own terms. How long until morning?"

"About eight hours. Why?"

He trembled. "I can rest during the day. At night I have to keep moving."

"You should be safe here. I have a cardboard box that would keep your light in."

"That was well meant, but I'm a hare, not a rabbit. I have to be able to see and hear around me, otherwise I get very nervous."

"Don't you sleep?"

"A few minutes at a time, during the day. That's instinctual but also necessary, if you glow. But I find I have to forage during the day, too. I haven't been able to stop moving at night long enough to eat."

"Okay. Do you know who this is?" I showed him the card picture.

He shivered harder. "Craig. Dr. Craig Morton. He's the one who said I should be terminated. Janet argued about that and he told her that she might not be around much longer, either. I assume he meant fired; I haven't seen any humans killed except on TV. But Janet was gone the next day and her desk in the lab corner was still full of stuff."

So, I had a missing scientist, an illegal or at least protocol-skirting gene lab, and an intelligent hare in jeopardy for its life and needing a refuge. It was, I figured, time to visit Dick Princeton. First, though, I had a bag of those bite-sized carrots in my cooler. I got it out and offered one to Jack. "Rabbit food, I know. But it's all I've got." I ate one myself.

"It will do. I'm very hungry."

I SENT an email Dick's way, packed up the next morning, was on my way east with Jack. Dick lives on a ridge on a private road uphill west of Mill Creek Road, just outside the Park. He's got a couple single-wides with a roof between them and a couple of prefab storage buildings in a clearing on the hilltop—home to a home-built radio telescope, an optical telescope, and all manner of electronic experiments.

Halfway up the road, Jack shuddered and jumped down to the van's floor.

A minute later a turkey vulture buzzed us and rocked its wings. We were expected. Once again, I marveled at Jack's sight and hearing.

"That's not a real vulture, Jack. It's, Dizzy, a drone Dick made to look like one."

"A vulture? I can see it now, but my instincts said 'eagle.' Do vultures ever attack like that?"

"Hmm. We'll have to talk to Dick about that; could be a giveaway. People aren't supposed to know about Dizzy."

"Can Dizzy, see as well as a real eagle or vulture?"

"Better. His optical resolution is only a little better, but it covers everything from UV to near infrared."

"Could...he find Dr. Janet?"

"That's what I'm going to ask Dick."

⁂

DICK AND SARAH came out to greet us. Sarah and Jack seemed to hit it off immediately. She bent down to shake Jack's right front foot, which he offered by standing as tall as he could, which was about four feet, ear tips to toes.

Dick's summer dining room was a picnic table between the two single-wides. I'd brought the carrots. Jack told us about his genetic modifications.

"They were trying brain densification—more neurons per cubic centimeter—to see if it would increase hare intelligence. In the next lab, they were working on human brain structure replacement cores, grown in animal hosts, for treatment of stroke victims and some developmental disorders. What happened next was complicated..."

Jack related what he'd told me, in somewhat more detail. "...so I have hundreds of times the number of synapses you have and in a millionth the volume—less communication distance, so faster." Jack twitched his ears. "My hearing is as good as you might guess; once I figured out English, I could tune into any conversation in the building and to maybe a couple hundred meters around. To a first approximation, I've learned what a state-of-the-art genetically modified organism researcher knows and remember it better."

"Including a lot of human personal life," I guessed.

Jack sighed. "Inevitably. I also know that they want me back before anyone else finds out what they did. They intend to terminate me."

"Do they know you are, uh, aware?"

"Yes. But not how much aware. They think I'm about at the level of Koko the gorilla or Alex the parrot, who were much discussed in my presence. They thought about keeping me around, but publishing the research on me would involve admitting their mistake. I played dumb bunny until my caretaker vanished a couple of days ago. Then I took the first opportunity to escape that came along. Now there is a small army with night vision goggles looking for me. They don't really need the goggles. I'm terrified, and hungry."

"You're equipped to forage and shelter in the wild," Dick said. "We can do it, too, but it's uncomfortable, time consuming, and takes a lot of work." He looked at me, "Even for those who think it's fun."

I chuckled.

Jack's nose twitched. "Typical hares live for maybe two or three years in their natural habitat. We can live a dozen or so with humans. My problem is that, despite all of this brain power, I have no learned experience for being a hare in the wild. I don't know what all I can eat. Another problem is that I'm constantly driven by all the evolutionary fears and appetites of a male jackrabbit. I can resist them, but it requires constant and exhausting vigilance." He trembled as he spoke, with his eyes fixed on Sarah.

I couldn't read the expression on Sarah's face. Jack was soft, cuddly, lovable, and he glowed. You wouldn't think twice about putting him on your lap, stroking, scratching and tickling him. But he had a mind, a voice, and was male to an extent that I probably couldn't comprehend. Nor could I comprehend how that package might affect Sarah, or affect Dick watching it affect Sarah.

If any of this human drama were affecting Jack (and why should it?) he gave no sign but just kept quivering and talking.

"My modifications were before differentiation; they affect my sperm; my offspring might not be as smart as I am, but they would be quite effective at evading predators and denuding the landscape. So it would be very irresponsible for me to mate with other lagomorphs. But mating with another species with the right chemistry could be exciting and might not be so dangerous."

"Who took care of you at the lab?"

Jack's ears twitched. "Jessica... no, Janet. Dr. Janet Jones. She made me a nice yard outside the lab that they kept planted with grass and bushes and a deep warm soft nest. I'm pretty sure it had a camera on it, but I couldn't figure out where it was."

"Did you get books," I asked, and light to read them?" Everyone, including Jack stared at me. "Oops. Sorry."

"I can't turn that off, either," Jack said. "I did my reading surreptitiously, on a monitor, or cage papers, or from Janet's lap. I miss her."

"Poor bunny," Sarah said, her voice full of compassion. She picked him up and cradled him in her arms. Something passed between Dick and Sarah.

Dick shrugged and smiled. "Ed, let's see about getting some intel on the GMO compound. We'll get Dizzy and Bizzy both on it."

Dizzy was his ornithopter drone turkey vulture. "Bizzy?" I asked.

"Dizzy Mark Two, with bigger batteries and a faster brain. It looks less suspicious if there are two of them, acting like buzzards. Come on. We should be back in a couple of hours or so, Sarah."

She smiled, stroking Jack. "No problems. Jack and I have something to do. We'll be back about 8 pm."

I imagined I could see his glow even in the day lit room. I gave them a quick smile and followed Dick out the door.

"She started out as a bio major and added the geology later," Dick said as we hoofed it up to the baseball-diamond sized hilltop clearing where Dick's equipment sheds were. The robot vultures stood like gargoyle statues beside a shed under its overhang.

"Igor?" Igor was Dick's home-built computer system that ran his single-wides, sheds, and anything else Dick wanted it to do.

"Yes, Dick?"

"Open the shed door and also check the Tri-City police departments for missing person reports for a Dr. Janet Jones.

"There are none."

It took only milliseconds. I was impressed.

"Hmm, Igor, find her home address and give it to Dizzy and Bizzy and have them make video. Off you go, guys."

The vultures walked over to the center of the green and, with a few soft flaps, they were on their way.

<hr>

DIZZY AND BIZZY got back a couple of hours later. We went over the video. There was no sign of Dr. Jones, but... I hit the pause icon.

"Dick, that's the rangy guy, one of the hunters that questioned me."

"Who's that with him? I've seen him, somewhere. Let's get a face recognition window over him."

In less than a minute, we had our answer. "It's Dr. Craig Morton, the guy on the card Rangy gave me. To the right with the gun," I added, "that's Heavy."

Dick grunted. "So all that talk about just being a low on the totem pole hunter under a contract to middlemen, etcetera, was B.S. He's working directly for Morton."

"Looks like," I said.

Dick and I kept at the vulture's video until Sarah and Jack showed up.

"Find something?" Sarah asked.

Dick explained and played back the video.

"Stop!" Sarah said. "She pointed to a sunlit face in an open door on the north side of the largest building. "Is that Dr. Jones? It looks like she's taking a smoke break."

Some of the smoke happened to drift out the door into the sunlight.

"Missed that," Jack said. "Let me try to get a spectrum on that." Dick said. A couple minutes later, he stroked his beard and said, "Ayup, *not* tobacco. Face recognition time."

It was indeed Dr. Janet Jones. She was smoking pot.

"Nervous, maybe?" I asked.

Dick laughed. He looked the classic sixties hippie. But to the best of my knowledge, he didn't drink, shoot, smoke or gamble, and never had. "Boots on the ground time," he said. "Ed, Think could you get in there?"

I'm a sometime science journalist, and was already part of this. It could be perfectly reasonable for me to show up on their doorstep.

"Maybe. Could Dizzy take Jack in and out?" I asked.

"Jack's a big, well-fed hare," Sarah said, "maybe four kilos. I think all Dizzy can lift is two or maybe three."

Dick nodded, but with that far off look that said his head was elsewhere.

"Okay. Jack," I asked, "are you willing to go in with me? You're much better built for snooping."

Jack shook like a leaf.

"Janet may need you," Sarah said.

"I can do it." Jack said. "Let's show them what we did."

"First we need to turn the lights out," she said.

With the lights out, Jack glowed. But then Sarah covered Jack with something that blocked the glow, except for maybe a trickle of light where the covering touched the floor.

"It's a bunny suit!" Dick said.

"More like a hare suit," Jack said, emitting a slight glow as he talked.

"Okay, Jack, jump!" Sarah commanded, when our eyes had night-adapted to the point where we could see what was happening, however dimly.

Jack jumped almost to the ceiling. His glowing hind legs flashed briefly on the way down.

"Laminated graphene," Sarah said. "I just printed it an hour ago; it's very thin. The eye holes and mouth holes were tricky. I had to leave the hind legs unencumbered; it's like the rabbit...er hare, equivalent of a hooded bathrobe, but it should work."

"I can go out to dinner!" Jack exclaimed. "Sarah showed me what I can eat."

"Okay," Dick said. "But stay around the clearing. I'll have Dizzy and Bizzy on the shed roofs as lookouts. As long as they don't have to fly, they can stay there all night on batteries."

While Jack foraged, we made plans for the next day.

I CONTACTED THE LAB. I'd done a *Popular Aerospace* article on bioengineered birds about a decade ago and used that, and Dr. Morton's card image, as 'credentials' and got an appointment with a Halfast information officer, an appropriately named Miss Twitter. I'd get a sanitized tour and maybe a few minutes with Dr. William Koglitz, Halfast's COO, if he had time, and Dr. Morton. They said they normally wouldn't do this on such short notice, but, as I hoped, Dr. Morton had recognized the name and wanted to talk to me.

Sarah came with me as my assistant. Her story, if they asked, was that she was moonlighting—learning the trade. In reality, I had more to learn from her.

We rode in her car, a clean, shiny, respectable late model Ford—one of a paleontologist's jobs these days was putting the bite on wealthy donors. Jack rode in the back seat, in a white version of the hare suit, with a pink ribbon around his neck next to a toy piano and a Nerf ball, equipped with an audiovisual collar that communicated, spread spectrum, with the robot vultures in KVVK's frequency slot. If you tuned into Las Amazonas, you'd be getting slightly more than you tuned in for, but wouldn't know it. Probably illegal, I thought, but Dick's philosophy was what the feds didn't know wouldn't hurt him.

The plan was to park on the far side of the lot on the south side of the admin building with the right door facing south, away from the surveillance camera. Jack would ditch the white hare suit in the back seat, slip under the driver's seat and, when Dizzy said the coast was clear, push the door open—Sarah would leave it ajar when she left with me—and hide until we left. Then he would find Janet, determine and record her status, and meet us in the lot; I would leave one of Dick's cell surplus phones 'accidentally' and need to return their retrieve it.

It worked like clockwork up through the interview with Dr. Koglitz, a very nice elderly European gentleman, who was enthusiastic about the prospects of genetic engineering to cure all sorts of things, but spoke in generalities with a lot of we'll-need-to-get-back-to-yous on details. At the end of our short talk, I asked how they make their test subjects glow.

"I've never asked, actually. Putting bioluminescent genes in to show that something is actually there and replicating has been done for many years now, all over. It's standard technology that doesn't hurt the subject animal. That we do, and we also do this to help recover any escaped animals—we don't want them to breed with the outside population. That would make difficulties with patented genes, you see. But the details on how we make them glow I do not know. We will get back to you. I'm sure it is harmless."

Harmless unless you're are a nocturnal critter outside the fence that needs to eat and not be eaten.

"Have there been other escapes?"

"Other than LLc 924? Ja. We have recovered them all. And it we will recover. We do not endanger the natural gene pool, that would not be in our interest or nature's, ja?"

I nodded.

"Oh, Dr. Molton has had to cancel. Perhaps you can come another day?"

"Certainly," I said, feigning slight disappointment. I was not surprised Molton canceled; I had no information on glowing rabbits and was taking info rather than giving.

He smiled broadly and looked at his watch. "It has been so nice talking to you, Herr Miller. Have a good evening."

The look on Sarah's face as I exited Koglitz' office told me something had gone wrong. She pointed to a company picture in the sitting area in the wide hall outside Dr. Koglitz's office. It showed Dr. Morton with Dr. Jones' arm around him and a big smile on her face. She texted it to Dick with the one word title "Trap!!" and showed the text.

"Get out of there!" Dick texted back. "I verified Jones and Morton are a couple; they're working together to get Jack She's bait. Plan B on extracting Jack."

Plan B?

Sarah froze and didn't seem to want to move.

"Let's work on having only two captives instead of four," I whispered. "We can always call the cops."

"Terrible coverage out here," someone said, noting our consternation and not knowing the cause. "You need to get halfway to Kiona before you get more than two bars."

"Thanks much," I said, and tugged on Sarah's hand, as the someone talked urgently on his phone.

She seemed to snap out of it and came along. My heart pounding, and my eyes looking this way and that for Heavy or Rangy and instant death, we walked to the car. This was a look into Jack's life, I realized, and it wasn't pretty. I'd hoped Jack would be there in the car—he should have gotten Sarah's warning, too. But the empty white bunny suit and lack or response to our calls said he wasn't there.

I put a sweaty palm on the passenger side door handle. "We can't wait," I told Sarah. "Dick has a Plan B. We need to get out of here and trust that."

She nodded and drove. I happened to glance in the back seat and look at the collapsed white toy bunny suit. If the same guys checked us on the way out.... I pulled off my shirt and my undershirt, put the shirt back on, and wadded the undershirt into the white bunny suit as Sarah rigorously followed the fifteen mph speed limit of the parking lot all the way to the exit gate.

We were searched. The bunny suit was squeezed, but not opened, or sniffed, and we were allowed out the gate. One turn down the road, out of view of Halfast, Sarah pulled the car over.

"You need to drive, Ed," she said, got out, and sat in back next to the empty bunny suit. I think she was trying hard not to cry.

I drove down to our rendezvous with Dick's van. Dick was in the cabin in front of a monitor, typing furiously.

"He doesn't respond to me. There doesn't seem to be anything wrong with the link. The feed's on DP734. You can watch with your cells. Sarah, did he tell you anything, any big secret, anything at all that might help?"

Sarah climbed in and put her hands on Dick's shoulders.

"Nothing that meant anything to me. Jones' name for Jack was 'Roger,' and she had him call her 'Jessica.' Why would he want to keep that secret?"

Sarah was born about 1992.

Dick could take care of that, I thought; I watched the feed. The hare cam showed the outside of the building we'd seen Dr. Jones in. Jack was stationary.

Dick sighed. "Sarah, google 'Jessica Rabbit.'"

She did so. "Oh...interspecies...she couldn't let that be known. Even if it means Jack's death, I guess. Dick, he's not a legal human being, not a person; he has no rights. The worst they could get for shooting him is cruelty to animals, or hunting without a license, or destroying evidence, or something."

"Yeah," I said. "Hold on, something's happening."

The building door opened. Jack covered the distance very quickly, then stopped by a jackrabbit-colored tarp and froze. If he just stayed there, he would be pretty much invisible.

"Sarah, Dr. Jones is the bait of the trap and Jack's rabbit reproductive instincts are fully engaged. I bet they've got the right pheromones wafting out that door too; it is a GMO lab. What we've got against that is Jack's mind and his instinctive caution. We need to tip the balance. Call him. Say it's you or Dr. Jones."

Sarah nodded. "Dick, what do I tell him besides 'don't go in'? What's plan B?"

"Run for the fence and jump as high as he can. About forty feet before the fence should do it."

Jack started to move toward the open door.

"Jack, it's Sarah. You're going into a trap. Janet isn't who you think she is."

"It's the only home I've ever known. She loves me…"

"No, she used you. You need to come to me. Run to the fence and jump high, to spoil their aim. Come to me," Sarah said. "Not her, me."

A tentative move toward the door, then a freeze.

"Rangy, with a shot gun, to the left," Dick said, watching Dizzy's feed. "Listen, Jack."

"Come to me," Sarah said.

Suddenly, Jack turned and started bounding down the lane between the buildings.

"Bizzy, eagle mode," Dick said. "Catch Jack on the the way up. Toss him over the fence. Dizzy, defend Jack. Jack, Jump! High as you can Jump!"

"Dick, Jack's too heavy. Bizzy won't be able to lift him."

"Doesn't have to. He just has to push his apogee up a bit."

The blast of a shotgun echoed from our phones and dust kicked up well ahead of Jack. Jack kept running, bouncing side to side now.

"I'm above to the left," a new voice said. It must be Bizzy, I realized. "Dodge to your left toward the fence and jump as high as you can."

There was another blast, dust far to the right of Jack, and then a human scream. "Help, get this thing off of me!"

"That would be Dizzy," Dick said.

The fence came in view. Jack dodged toward it, jumped, and kept on soaring. Later, we figured he and Bizzy cleared the fence by twenty-two feet, three and one half inches.

BACK AT DICK'S place that evening, Jack performed his experiment with a bit of Black Butte Porter in a bowl.

"It tastes awful," he said.

"I could make some chamomile tea," Sarah offered.

Jack took another sip of Porter. "Maybe I'll learn to like it. As I like my new home."

We all laughed and cheered.

"I've got good news for you, Jack, from Halfast Lab. They actually got back to me; the reason you glow is GM bioluminescent bacteria in your epidermal biome. We need to kill all the bugs on your skin hair and replace them with the normal variety. Then you won't glow."

Igor interrupted us with a KVVK report, from FAUX news, that "…a pair of eagles had interrupted a rabbit hunt on the grounds of Hanford. Their expert said that wasn't usual eagle behavior—they would more likely to fight each other for the prey than cooperate—but that strange biological things had been reported at Hanford. Jackrabbits eat contaminated plants, glow

in the dark and so on. This was all unconfirmed of course, but you heard it first on..."

Sarah laughed, Jack secure on her lap. "You won't find one person in ten that can tell the difference between a turkey vulture and a golden eagle in flight at a quick glance. Most people go by behavior; eagles don't rock their wings or gather in big groups over road kill. Casual observers don't get a good look at the head, nor, of course, inside it. Dizzy and Bizzy flew like eagles today."

Yes, I thought. And everyone else around me got "up where they belong," too.

To Plant or Pull Up Stakes

JOYCE REYNOLDS-WARD

"Quit!" Peter McLoughlin snapped at his black and white spotted Palouse gelding, Feather, as he pranced in front of one of the cairns that marked the magical Line protecting the Oregon Country. Like too many of the signposts they had seen today, this one had scattered stones around it, as if something had knocked them free, weakening the magic foundation of the Line.

Feather snorted, pawing the ground, then looked uphill at their companions, Jesse and Henawit, whose horses and the pack mule carefully picked their way down the steep, rocky slope from the last cairn.

"Good boy," Peter said, rubbing the gelding's midnight-black neck. He couldn't blame Feather. These half-scattered cairns set his teeth on edge. It felt like a wild unicorn bent on destroying magic not of its creation. That *wrong feeling* sent chills down his back on this hottest of summer days, when the desert sun should be making him sweat.

There shouldn't be any unbonded wild unicorns left in the Oregon Country.

That suggested a greater breach than the original one from last winter.

Henawit, Peter's Nimiipuu magical mentor, rode up next to him while Jesse wrestled with their pack mule. "More of the same."

"The magic feels like a unicorn."

"What does Feather tell you?" Henawit asked. He had trained the black gelding with the white blanket covered with black spots on his rump to be a unicorn-fighting horse. He gave Feather to Peter after last winter, when Peter rode Feather alongside the footloose witch Hilda Solanas against spies from the Mission Board, the tool of the unified Union and Confederate forces against the Country.

"I smell the stink of a witch along with the unicorn," Jesse Grubb growled as he wrangled the pack mule close to this particular marker. "At least that's what *I* say."

"Young Jesse, those traces are inconclusive and mixed," Henawit said. "Here." He dismounted. "Come with me. I'll show you why we can't be certain."

Jesse hesitated, looking at the mule. "This pig-headed thing wants to run off."

"*Whoa*," Henawit said firmly, flicking a finger at the mule. A yellow spark lit on the mule's lead. "Drop the lead, Jesse. He won't move now."

"I've got to figure out that magic," Jesse muttered. "Especially with a cantankerous beast like this one."

"Practice," Henawit said serenely. "Lots of it."

Peter hid the smile that threatened to break free. Was it only a year since he'd been in Jesse's position? Jesse was one of the Applegate clan's best developing young magicians, but compared to Henawit and Peter, he was no more than a beginner. Henawit was one of the strongest Nimiipuu shamans, had participated in the early formation of the Line twenty years ago.

The three of them carefully restacked the stones in the cairn. Then they joined hands, Henawit leading them in a chant that made the cairn flare a bright yellow-white, then transition to a steady blue glow before Henawit masked it again.

Peter left Henawit and Jesse behind to administer the final touches as he rode to the next marker, checking Feather when the gelding would have trotted down the rocky slope. This pillar was special, halfway down the stretch of the Line that bisected the Watch Mountains and the desert basin below. A faint smudge of green in the basin marked Dugout Hot Springs, their destination for the night. This southeastern corner of the Line was the most isolated portion except for the existence of Dugout, which contained one of the shielded portals that allowed emigrants to enter the Oregon Country.

Jesse followed by Henawit joined Peter at this pillar, a solid chunk of lava instead of the multi-rock cairns that were the usual markers. "The Line feels funny here."

"It's solid," Peter said. This was where he and Hilda Solanas had joined forces to seal out last winter's supernatural incursion. *Where are you now, Hilda?* Until they'd worked that magic together he'd disliked the woman. But now—he knew more about the circumstances that had driven her actions. Not that she was welcome here. Magic within the Country required oaths and licensing, a form of control that the Outside lacked. He didn't think Hilda was ready for that.

"It feels like something from the Outside worked magic," Jesse pressed, setting his jaw stubbornly.

"This is part of the Line I repaired last winter. It is solid." *Sealed by the power of the McLoughlins and the blood of the witches of Salem. A son of Salem and of the Country.*

Jesse's jaw jutted out stubbornly. "Then why does it reek of *that witch?*"

"What witch?" Peter asked, struggling to keep his voice steady. How could Jesse identify Hilda's mark in the magic they had used to mend the Line here?

"I don't know her name," Jesse muttered. "But I know the stink of her magic! White and Lee sent her after us, like a bull-baiting dog she was. Chased us almost all the way here from Morning Sun after they routed us out in the Confederacy's name."

White and Lee. Henawit raised a brow at Peter. Peter nodded, understanding what Henawit meant. The malign spirit in the pillar was contained there as the result of Hilda and Peter's work, which had thwarted White and Lee's goals. Hilda had been an enslaved witch forced to comply with the Mission Board's attempt to pry open the Oregon Country for missionary incursions as the first wave of a joint Union-Confederate invasion. Mending that breech with Peter had freed Hilda and thwarted the Mission Board's schemes.

"There was a witch who contributed to building this section of the Line," Peter said slowly. "But she was under bond at the time, and earned her freedom as part of her labor. You have a problem with that, or the working she did?"

"Under bond, you say?" Jesse's jaw eased slightly, though still with a trace of that stubbornness.

"She helped rebuild the Line of her own free will and earned freedom as a result of her efforts. Then she left the Country."

Jesse chewed on his lower lip for a moment. "All right. Despite her taint, and the life she owes to my family, I'll let it stand. For now."

Good. "Why don't you two ride ahead to the next marker? I need to make certain the spirit we imprisoned in this one is still contained, and I'd just as soon not expose you two to it."

Henawit nodded curtly and gestured to Jesse.

Peter waited until they had ridden downslope to the next cairn, Jesse straining to keep the mule from pulling ahead, before he dismounted. Feather raised his head and shifted the bit nervously in his mouth, sending soft vibrations down the reins to Peter's hand. Peter rested a hand on Feather's neck.

"Only a moment," he whispered soothingly to the gelding. "I need your help."

Feather twitched his ears forward, and snorted at the pillar. Peter took a shorter hold on the reins and put one hand on the stone. The spirit within roiled, lashing out with a sharp white-hot edge at his palm. Peter forced the edge back. *Blood of the McLoughlins, Blood of the Line,* he thought. *You shall not prevail.*

The binding held. The spirit sulked back into the base of the pillar, grumbling and muttering but no longer resistant. A fresh whisper of Hilda's lavender and sage scent tickled Peter's nose.

Show me, he demanded of the spirit. It grumbled, then gave him a quick flash of Hilda standing in the same place as him, seeking—what?—dropping onto her knees before the pillar. A darker-skinned man with similar features as hers stood further back, holding two horses.

Peter probed further. But he found no signs of tampering. To all appearances, Hilda had done no more than what he was doing now—stopped to ensure that malign spirit was still bound.

Peter swung up on Feather. The gelding eagerly picked up a trot, then a gallop, as soon as Peter settled in the saddle. Peter let him run, happy to get away from that one pillar. Most likely Hilda had moved on from here, seeking whatever mischief called her name. He couldn't tell when it was she had been there, just that she had been there sometime this summer.

Still, as Peter rejoined Henawit and Jesse, the lingering sense of her presence nagged at him.

Despite his confident words to Henawit and Jesse, he could still sense that unicorn. The combination of Hilda and unicorn worried him. She had once been a Confederate unicorn rider. Once settled in for the night he'd check the edge on his unicorn-killing machete tucked into the mule's pack.

Might be a good idea to carry it again.

THE LAST RAYS of sunlight faded behind them as they rode into Dugout Hot Springs. The stage stop was little more than a cluster of stable; two small cabins; a larger building that served as inn, saloon and brothel; and the enclosure around the hot springs. Two tall pillars flanked by long walls of rocks marked the entrance through the Line that Pauline maintained. The approaching dusk made the entrance screen meant to capture witches for Pauline's approval shine with a faint blue shimmer. Otherwise, the Line was invisible, save to magicians like Peter, Henawit, and Jesse.

They stopped by the stable first.

"Busy night, McLoughlin," the hostler commented, using Peter's name as a title. "Got a lot of passers-through."

"Oh?" Peter noticed the fine gray gelding in the stall closest to them. It looked similar to the gray that Hilda's companion had been holding in his vision at the pillar.

"Couple of miners, handful of cowboys riding back from driving cows to the railroad at Winnemucca."

"Think there'll be room at the inn?"

"Cowboys aren't staying, just stopping for a quick bite and maybe a drink. Miners seemed more interested in the girls. Might be some competition there."

Jesse flushed. Peter shrugged. "Rooms, dinner, and a bath. That's all we're looking for."

"We do have one other odd pair here tonight who seemed interested in the Line's status. Red-haired woman with a black man who's not a servant or slave. She called him her brother. Couldn't tell by their skin color, though features look similar."

Chills ran down Peter's spine. "Did you get a name for the woman?"

The hostler shook his head. "I know better than to poke into witch's business, and that redhead is certainly a witch."

"I'm surprised Pauline allowed the witch entrance into the Country without proof of her oath. Normally she is strict about the rules."

"The witch was already in the Country," the hostler said. "Came from the same direction you did. Showed the approval token to Pauline, so Pauline didn't throw her out. Pauline seemed real interested in talking to her though."

Peter noticed that Jesse's hands clenched into fists. "I thank you for the information." He dropped an extra gold coin into the hostler's palm. "It's been useful."

Jesse marched next to Peter on the way to the saloon. "If she's that witch, I've sworn by my honor as a Grubb and an Applegate that she will pay for what she did to us."

"There may be more to the story than you know," Peter said.

"Man, she drove my family out of Iowa!"

"From what I see, your family were already fiddle-foots looking for any excuse to pull up stakes to find a greener horizon," Peter said mildly.

"We're not you high and mighty McLoughlins," Jesse countered. "Farmer's luck busted us out of that Iowa farm. Which wasn't helped by her witchcraft."

"She may not have been operating under her own initiative," Henawit said, coming up on Jesse's other side. "When we encountered Miss Solanas last winter, she was bound to White and Lee." Henawit jerked his head toward Peter. "*He* got rid of that."

Jesse muttered something under his breath.

"Remember that you're here to learn about mending the Line so you can help maintain it. As such, you owe the lady respect. By her actions last winter she became as much a servant of the Line as you are," Henawit said sternly.

"Don't like it," Jesse grumbled louder.

"We all have to do things we'd much rather not do," Henawit said. "She killed my band's chief at the Battle of John Day. If anyone is owed vengeance, my people are." He fixed Jesse with a stern glance. "I've chosen not to take that opportunity because of what she's done since. You hear me?"

"Yes," Jesse said, withering under Henawit's glare.

"Good. See that you remember it."

They went into the saloon.

"Mr. McLoughlin! How pleasant to see you again!" Pauline rose from the small table where she sat with a redheaded woman and a darker-skinned man who resembled the one Peter had glimpsed in his brief contact with the pillar. *Hilda's brother?*

"You're looking good, Miss Pauline," Peter said, kissing her on the cheek. "Do you have room for three of us plus baths?" At the sound of his voice, Hilda turned to look at the three of them. She flushed and turned away, leaning over to talk to the dark man.

"Always room for you and Henawit," Pauline said, turning to Henawit next, shaking his hand. "And who is this?" She looked Jesse up and down appraisingly. "On business of the Line?"

"Yes. Jesse Grubb, ma'am," Jesse said, holding out his right hand.

" From Ashland or Jacksonville?" Pauline asked.

"Ashland," he said.

"Samuel or William's son?"

"William's," Jesse said. "Samuel is my grandfather."

Pauline nodded and took Jesse's hand in hers. "Welcome to Dugout, young Jesse Grubb. How fares Old Applegate?"

"He's doing well," Jesse said.

"Young Jesse here is apprenticing to the Line," Peter said. "In place of Meek, who's decided to manage the law in Oregon City."

"I'll miss old Joe but I'm glad to see you've got the Applegates working on the Line," Pauline said. "Ashland is closer than Oregon City."

"Have there been further problems?" Peter asked.

"Nothing obvious, nothing big. I've had some—*interesting*—

conversations with Miss Hilda here," Pauline said. "Peter McLoughlin, Henawit, Jesse Grubb, this is Hilda Solanas."

Hilda and her companion rose as they reached the table. Hilda extended her hand to Peter.

"We've met, Miss Pauline. So good to see you again, Peter McLoughlin," she said.

Peter kissed her hand. "Always a pleasure, Miss Solanas. I thought you had left the Oregon Country for good?"

Hilda grimaced. "Alas, there are matters that forced my return." She gestured to the dark man. "May I introduce my brother, David Solanas?"

"Mr. Solanas." Peter took David's hand, noticing that it was firm and hard, the hand of a man accustomed to physical labor. "So what brings you here?"

Hilda glanced warily at the cowboys. "Perhaps we could talk privately?" She nodded at Henawit. "Good to see you, Henawit." Then she frowned as she looked at Jesse Grubb, who glowered at her. "Do I know you? You seem familiar."

"You should recognize me!" Jesse spluttered. "You drove us out of Morning Sun! Cursed my family! How could you not know us?"

Hilda raised her brows. "Grubb, Grubb, I don't remember that name." She coughed.

"He's Applegate kin," Peter interjected. "By marriage."

Hilda flinched. "Oh dear." She sighed. "Does it help that I was not in command of myself at the time of your family's unfortunate involvement with my masters?"

"Witch," Jesse hissed. "You cursed us."

Hilda sighed. "And the curse died with my release from White's and Lee's bondage. Or at least it should have. Young Mr. Grubb, I am so sorry for what I had to do. I would make amends—but other matters take precedence. All I can do is ask for your forgiveness."

Jesse scowled. "Not me you need to speak to."

"I will give you something for Old Applegate later," Hilda said. She turned back to Peter. "That talk."

"Can we do so after a bath and dinner?" Peter asked.

"Perhaps we could join you for dinner?" She turned to Pauline. "Would that be doable?"

"Certainly. All of you or just the two of you?"

"All of us," Peter said.

Much as he wanted to meet with Hilda privately, wisdom dictated otherwise.

"All right," Pauline said briskly. "You know which rooms to use, Peter. I'll have Eliza lay out towels at the spring and wash your dirties."

"I thank you," Peter said. "Both of you."

"Pshaw! Anything for the Line," Pauline said.

Peter picked up his possibles bag and nodded at Hilda and David. "We will speak soon," he said.

Hilda smiled wistfully at him. "Until then."

A SOAK and wash in the hot springs, followed by a shave and changing into the set of good non-work clothing in his bag, made Peter feel almost as polished and elegant as he would be in Oregon City. Eliza guided them to the private parlor in the back that Pauline often reserved for special occasions.

Hilda, David, and Pauline already waited at the table. They settled in with the first course, minestrone with fine wheat biscuits, served with a flask of burgundy. No sooner had Eliza left the room after serving than Hilda set down her spoon.

"Fortunate that I encountered you this quickly," she said. "Changes ride the wind, McLoughlin," the solemnity of her tone making his name a title. "The Line must hold firm."

"What arises?" Peter asked. He sipped on his wine, staving off his disquiet.

Hilda and David exchanged glances. "I was slave to Harney of the Mission Board," David said. "The Board was concerned over reports of unusual—creatures in the Oregon Country. Above and beyond unicorns, that is. Rumors of dragons."

"The Confederates have their own tame dragons," Peter said, keeping his voice calm.

"Few wild dragons remain," Henawit said. "Gone, with the unicorns."

"Not flesh-and-blood dragons," David said. "The Confederates claim that the Oregon Country possesses mechanical airships."

"That is a matter to be discussed with the Peoples and their councils," Peter said. "The Shoshone in particular."

"Then the airships do exist."

"The magic is not for whites," Henawit said gruffly. "And not all the People operate the airships."

"That is not an answer that the Mission Board will accept," David said. "The Board, as the contact agency to subjugate Deseret, California, and Oregon, has decided to increase their evangelical efforts to defang the magic that keeps Oregon free from both Union and Confederate influence."

"Stone by stone, is what one of their agents said to us under questioning," Hilda said. "They threatened to destroy the Line stone by stone."

"Stones have been missing from the cairns we checked this afternoon," Peter said.

"Whereabouts?" Pauline asked.

"Descending from the Watch Mountains," Henawit said.

"More than normal attrition," Peter said. "But I don't think that it was human hands that did it."

"You said there were no more wild unicorns in the Oregon Country," Hilda said. "What I've sensed reeks of unicorn."

"No bound unicorn with the ability to tamper with the cairns has come in through *my* portal," Pauline said. "And the Line protects the cairns from Outside attack."

"The unicorn may have been here a while. He did attempt to attack the spirit pillar," Hilda said. "We had swung over from the Sand Creek Mountains, tracking what I could feel of the unicorn's trail." She waved her hand toward the mountain range on the other side of the basin from the Watches. "Entered at the Corners and did spot checks along the Line there. We couldn't reach all of the cairns. Something repelled us."

"Why?" Peter asked.

"I wish I knew," Hilda said, frowning. "I didn't use much effort, because it's a distraction. David needs refuge because of what he knows from his enslavement at the Mission Board."

"We've been riding like hell for the Oregon Country ever since Hilda helped me escape," David added. "I'm hoping my information will be useful."

"It sounds useful enough to me," Peter said. "How far ahead of the Mission Board's slave hunters are you? Could we make them think that David is spying on the Shoshone as a double agent to investigate the Board's concerns?"

Hilda shook her head. "Too far-fetched."

"Not a rationale they would accept," David said. "Not without prior arrangement."

"Another possibility. If you are sworn to service in the Oregon Country then the Mission Board has no claim on you," Peter said. "We need to repair those segments of the Line you just told me about, Hilda. With your magic, we can get through the process much more quickly and get David to Oregon City."

The faint noise of raised voices, followed by gunshots, came from outside. Pauline stood.

"There's trouble at the portal," she said. "How far behind did you say the Mission Board riders were?"

"Close enough," Hilda said. "We've got to hide David!"

"No we don't," Peter said as Pauline left the room. "David. Will you swear to service in the Oregon Country?"

"What would my duties be?"

"The care and feeding of magicians for one," Peter said. "Another hand to help with camp and water and cooking would be of great use. We'd ride the Line for another two months, then go back to Oregon City for the winter. At that point you have two months of service to the Country and no impediment to full citizenship. Sound good?"

David grinned. "Best deal I've got at the moment."

"Put your hand to mine." Peter waited until David's darker hand pressed against his. "Repeat after me. I, David Solanas, do solemnly vow to serve the Line and its workers, keeping all secrets and offering no aid or comfort to those who would see the Oregon Country destroyed."

David repeated the words. Peter felt the power stir within his palm.

"Should I betray the Oregon Country and the Line, may death find me painfully and quickly."

Peter waited. David repeated this part of the Oath unhesitatingly.

"So do I swear before the Peoples of the Oregon Country. I renounce all ties and linkages to any other nation. I vow the equality of all no matter what race. I will resist slavery, the blandishments of the old colonies, the money of the Crown, and any others who seek to conquer the Oregon Country. So help me God."

Peter tightened his fingers around David's. Closing his eyes, he visualized a bright fire washing over the two of them. David's hand clenched under Peter's, then relaxed.

The fire finished pulsing just as the door slammed open, admitting three men with pistols drawn, followed by two more men with rifles.

"Hand over that slave!" the scruffy man in the lead said.

"He is no slave, but sworn to the service of the Line and the Oregon

Country," Peter said.

The man gestured with his pistol toward Hilda and David. "Take them. Both of them."

"You are in violation of the Line!" Pauline bellowed from behind the men. "And as caretaker of the Dugout Hot Springs, I pronounce you exiled. Begone!"

She snapped her fingers. A golden thread wound around the men. But the lead man just snorted.

"My warrant from the Mission Board is slave-sworn and not subject to your witchery," he sneered, reaching into his shirt pocket. His smirk faded as he pulled out the paper. "It's gone! See where the mark was?" He pointed to a faint red stain where the Mission Board's magical seal had authorized him to take into custody one David Solanas, slave, and his sister Hilda Solanas, witch and slave.

Peter smiled humorlessly at the man. "Mr. David Solanas has been sworn to the service of the Oregon Country. His sister has also provided service to the Country. Your warrant does not hold when dealing with those who have become part of the Country. Now. Go." He put extra magical emphasis on the last word.

"Begone," Pauline repeated. "You have no power here. Leave the Country now."

The men protested as the guns vanished from their hands. Pauline's golden ribbon tightened around them, pulling them back and away from the door. Before the lead man disappeared, he shook his fist at Peter, David, and Hilda.

"You've not heard the last of me!" he bellowed. "You'll never be welcome in the Union or the Confederacy! We'll see to that!"

"Well!" Hilda said, sinking down into her chair once things became quiet. "It seems we've burned our bridges, David."

"If you're staying here, you've a life debt to my family," Jesse growled. "You may have made amends on the Country's level—but to us an obligation is owed."

"I will be helping to mend the Line—is that not sufficient?" Hilda asked Jesse.

"That will have to be a ruling by Old Applegate," he said.

Hilda looked at Peter. "I should be helping finish these fixes on the Line."

"Perhaps she and David could go back to Ashland with you once we're done with the Line for this season, Jesse," Peter suggested.

"There are some witches that need training," Jesse said.

"Then that will work."

They settled back down to dinner, no one speaking. After they ate, Hilda would have slipped away but Peter placed his hand on her arm.

"Care to step out and look at the sky?" he asked.

"We'll be seeing plenty of it while fixing the Line," she said. Nonetheless, Hilda took Peter's arm. The two of them went outside, standing on the wooden porch. The stars hung bright above.

But the stars were not Peter's focus. He studied the bright blue and white glow of the Line as it snaked up the Sand Creek Mountains.

"I really hadn't planned for me and David to end up here."

"Sometimes when you're pulling up stakes you don't know where you're going to plant them next," Peter said.

"Best-laid plans gone awry," she agreed, sighing.

"Summer on the Line. Winter with the Applegates. Have you any plans beyond that?"

Hilda shrugged. "By then perhaps I'll find another reason to move on."

"And your role with the Line? You are sworn to it after what we did last winter."

"Other things take precedence. That unicorn. It's waiting for me. Your country isn't going to accept me as a unicorn rider, no matter what role I've played in mending the Line. Not with the power I've sensed from that one."

"Perhaps it's time the Oregon Country learns to tolerate unicorn riders."

"Won't happen, not as long as the Union and Confederates use tame unicorns in war. And that unicorn—he needs me. Needs help to get to a safe place outside of the Country. I'd sure like to know how he got here. I'd thought your old unicorn hunters had wiped the wild ones out of the Oregon Country before the Line was laid down."

"They were supposed to have been. But maybe that one has something to do with the problems I sensed along the Line. It could have slipped within the boundary last winter."

"Could be." Hilda hesitated. "If we find it before winter, I may need to leave sooner rather than later. I doubt the Applegates will tolerate a unicorn rider in their midst."

"Let's wait and see what happens instead," Peter suggested.

A shooting star lit up the night sky and they watched it flare out in white and green light above the Watch Mountains. Hilda patted Peter's arm.

"I think it's best that you consider me as coming in and out of your life like that shooting star. Besides, if I can catch that unicorn and bond it to me?" She chuckled softly. "Let the Mission Board *think* I've seen the error of my ways. With a unicorn's support, no one can stop my magic or bind me again. Not after making a bond with it as a free woman. But they won't believe that. No one will stop to consider about the likelihood that I'm a double agent for the Oregon Country."

"Must you?"

Hilda was silent for a few minutes. When she spoke again, her voice was subdued and quiet.

"I got my brother free. But as long as slavery exists on Union and Confederate soil, I can't put down stakes anywhere." She patted Peter's arm again. "Sorry, Peter. But it's my duty."

"Then I guess I'll have to do my best to ensure that the Oregon Country does the right thing," he said. "Because whether you can hear me or not, Hilda Solanas—you've gotten into my blood, just like I know I've gotten into yours. And no amount of pulling up stakes on your part is going to change that. Sooner or later we'll be together."

"You dreamer." But there was gentleness rather than scoffing in her tone. "You could always come with me."

"I couldn't. I have too many responsibilities to the Oregon Country." He didn't add that his magic was bound to this land. He wasn't ready to risk that loss. Yet.

She laughed. "Those stakes bind you, Peter McLoughlin. Maybe it's time you thought about pulling them up." Hilda drew a deep breath. "It's getting late. Morning comes early and that stretch of the Line in the Sand Creeks is in a really hot location. We had best get started at or before daybreak. I think it's best that we retire for the evening."

"True," Peter conceded. They went inside, and went upstairs together, stopping outside of Hilda's room. "Just remember this," he said. "I will not give up easily."

She smiled at him. "You're a McLoughlin. I wouldn't expect anything else." Then she went inside her room.

Peter smiled to himself as he left her.

Sooner or later, Hilda would need to plant stakes somewhere. And when she did—he planned to be there.

Where ever that turned out to be.

Franklin

BRUCE TAYLOR

OK. I just wanna set the record straight. Yeah, maybe I was the last guy to see Franklin

Bills. I dunno. Maybe so. And I don't know what really became of him—in–um—how can I put it?—in *this* reality. But I wonder if this here's the only reality there is given what finally came into my head as to what maybe *did* happen to him and that's where this story gets a bit tough.

You see, it's like this—I knew Franklin maybe eight—nine years or so. He was a tall, kinda gangly, sandy-haired kid with a lot of freckles and wore glasses, never smiled much but, thanks to me, he was always carting around those science fiction magazines of the forties and fifties: *Galaxy, Fantasy & Science Fiction, Infinity.* I'm sure you know the ones I'm talkin' about. Even with new magazines coming out, nope, we were both readin' those old magazines. Maybe it was all that wild imagination, all that energy; after all, from '38 to '46, it was called The Golden Age of Science Fiction for a reason. Maybe, in part, it was me looking back with nostalgia at what the future was supposed to be like, while for Franklin the stories were like a universe of possibilities and a whole bunch of new ones—but those old magazines, always kinda the glue that held us together. I loved 'em. And Franklin? What can I say? He always had that wistful look after reading a story by Bradbury, H. G. Wells, Davidson or Blish, and you know, you know that was the world he wanted to live in. Yeah, loved those magazines and always, always that kinda lost and wistful look.

We got together often, starting in the mid-'60s, after he realized he loved science fiction almost as much as I did but there was a difference, of course. You gotta understand, I think I connected with him the way he and his pappy couldn't.

His folks had property right next to mine, in Eastern Washington, just outside the little town of Twisp, south on 92 from Winthrop. But his house was down the road a ways.

Now seemed to me, he never took much of a shine to his folks or maybe they never took that much of a shine to him. Don't get me wrong, everything was decent here, OK? Good people, easy goin' but sometimes, something is—must be—missing between parents and their kids. So maybe it's genetic, maybe somehow something skipped a generation, maybe the reincarnate in "reincarnation" lost an existential wheel. Who knows? Sadly, sometimes that's the way it is.

But I took a shine to him. *What a decent kid*, I always thought. *What a swell kid.* And after I lost my wife, God rest her soul, I guess it musta been about, lessee, 1964—yeah, I was in my early 30s. Boy, what a shock. Losin' Betty was just a sonofabitch. Cancer. Ovarian cancer did her in. Did the best we could. Local treatment when possible in Wenatchee, extensive treatment over in Seattle at the University Hospital. And while she was in treatment, I'd go over to the Pay n' Save there on Madison, just across the street from the old Washington Mutual Bank that later got all eaten up by the Great Recession of '08. That so few went to jail for all that blatant greed still disgusts me. But that's another story.

Anyway, I grew up on the great pulps of the early 40s and 50s featuring the up and coming stars of Science Fiction, be it Bradbury, Del Camp, A. E van Vogt, William F. Nolan, not to mention the classic works of H. G. Wells, Edgar Rice Burroughs, Jules Verne. Guess that's how I coped with what Betty was going through. Helped her as much as I could and wish, oh, God, *so* wish I could have done so much more. Met in high school. Love at first sight. And I'm here to tell ya yeah, love at first sight exists. Sure as hell does.

But anyway, that kinda helped me cope with it all and to Betty's credit, she took an interest in science fiction as well, especially Bradbury.

"He writes so well," she always said, her blue eyes glistening, "no matter how awful or difficult life can be, Bradbury provides solace, a bigger picture of life."

I knew a lot of his work early on and know that if he didn't explicitly say he believed in reincarnation, he sure hinted at it a lot. And maybe that's what helped Betty. God, it's amazing what one person can do to help another whom they don't know, never will, but by putting themselves out there, they do indeed inspire us and make the world a better place.

Now. What's all this got to do with Franklin? Like this. After Betty passed in early '65, well, it was just hard as hell to be at home. Even though we were right out of town and everything was still close by, I just had to get out every day and invariably, I'd run into Franklin. Yeah, musta been some twenty-odd years between us but in spite of my aches and pains, I'd still take a morning walk and I could see him coming out the door of his home maybe quarter mile 'way and I'd kinda slow down and let him close in on me.

First few times, he hung real far back so I thought, *OK, just mosey on my way.* So I'd head on over to the Twisp Bakery on Glover Street and by now, it was early spring, '65. I'd sit at the outside tables after getting my mail and every three or four weeks there would be a new *Galaxy*, *Infinity*, or something in the P.O. box. I would just sit outside with that super good coffee that Carla made up there in the bakery, and I tell you, it was like nectar. I'd sit out there and read the latest story by Bradbury, Silverberg, Bova, Nolan or Herbert but still carried with me old 1955 *Galaxy*s or something to reread a favorite story and to be honest, still preferred the stuff of the last couple of decades (Lord only knows *how* many times I read Godwin's *The Cold Equations*).

But finally one day, musta been mid-afternoon, I was reading and noticed out of the corner of my eye, someone had stopped. Looking up, it was Franklin. Obviously shy, yet, mesmerized by proposed cover art (a digest-sized image which I *always* carried with me; done and with personalized signature to me by my super artistic friend, Jack Hendricks, back a year or so for *Infinity Science Fiction*. They couldn't use it, which was really too bad, but it sure didn't stop Jack who went on to do cover art for other magazines anyway), and just had it out, like I usually do, on the table along with old copies of *If* and *Unknown.* It just drew him like a magnet. It was an illustration for a Bradbury story: a fanciful city on Mars, beside the blue waters of a broad canal and on the side of it, a Mars maiden I guess, dressed in a beautiful saffron robe, with reddish hair and faint orange skin, obviously with her feet in the water of that canal. Yeah, yeah, later that summer, the Mariner Probe would find the planet as a dead and pretty quiet place, but still, a fanciful cover of what so many hoped Mars might still be like. But after the probe in the summer of '65 saw the reality of Mars, well, Jack's proposed Mars cover for *Infinity* was now relegated to dreams. Jack later told me that he thought maybe the editors knew in advance the proposed art might be obsolete before long. But Franklin was spellbound by the now nostalgic and orphaned cover art.

I smiled, motioned to the chair and said, "Young fella, have a seat. I think it's about time we introduced each other properly, doncha think?"

So shy but he smiled and it was like his freckles became a couple of shades paler. But not saying anything, he sat.

He pointed to the illustration, and almost inaudibly he said, "Can I see?"

Well, not only did I let him admire that cover art, but I also let him look at a 1954 copy of *Galaxy.* Also in my stash of mail that I always picked up at the post office, there was a brand new *Fantasy & Science Fiction* with a wonderful cover of an alien beach with a double sun blazing in a aquamarine sky, and the list of jaw-dropping authors: Le Guin, Herbert, Asimov, and a sprinkling of names from the Golden Age.

He looked at the covers.

I smiled. *Hooked.*

He looked again at the proposed cover art with the Mars maiden.

"Chocolate ice cream cone?" I asked.

He abruptly looked up, nodded once, and then those hazel eyes again drank in that image that featured a fanciful Martian city and Mars maiden on the side of the canal. Finally he set down the art, then began to look at the other magazines with rapt attention.

Hooked. I smiled. *Hooked, hooked, hooked.*

Just about twice, three times a week, we'd end up at that table outside, and if it got too hot, or too cold, we'd be inside, me drinking coffee and having a roll and he having hot chocolate or ice cream. Sometimes we didn't say much to each other, just sat there reading. More often than not, when you are looking at something amazing or profound, you don't have to say a word. You just tap someone on the shoulder and point, or shove the story over to them and in minutes, they get it and you share something fantastic, amazing, even horrifying.

Yeah, favorite memories were the times the snows were deep in Twisp, and us sitting there in the bakery, watching the snow fall and the town lookin' as pretty as a Christmas card and—just us sitting there with coffee and Franklin with his hot chocolate and later, coffee. Those days, those days, what can I say about those days. No, Betty wasn't around and God knows I missed her like something God-awful. But then you can have other people in your life and there's all the reason in the world to live, to go on because the world continues to be such a fantastic place and worlds beyond this one and by dint of imagination, we explore them. Then we come back, we come back and I'd be slowly putting my coffee down as if suddenly remembering I'd been holding it as I read a story, or Franklin might be looking up after reading a story with that lost-in-wonder look. Guess that look kinda made up tor him not smiling much but anyway, how much better can it be? And outside, snowing like crazy, but inside, warm, cozy; the sound of silverware on tables, a laugh by Carla, the smell of coffee and toast and rolls and in all of this—wonder. Worlds of worlds beyond worlds and you came back to this one and it's more fantastic than ever.

Now this went on for maybe seven, eight years. And in all this time, strange as it seems, never really had much to do with Franklin's folks except the rare times I'd run into them. They were always polite, thanked me for being a pal to Franklin, but for the times I'd run into them to be *so* rare in a small town like Twisp, well that's probably something best left for a *Twilight Zone* episode, I guess. Or maybe a story in *Weird Tales*. Who knows.

But. Time moves on, and well, around about the time Franklin was in high school, I started seeing him less and less. That made me sad and kinda lonely all over again but I also knew that he was headin' toward graduation, then it was going to be off to someplace else. And through the years, he had learned to talk a bit more. Finally one time, which turned out to be the last time I saw him, he said, "Y'know, Drake, I've really come to say how much I've appreciated all the years we've spent doing this —never had much connection with my folks but—"

I looked at him, freckles faded away, hair still sandy, black-framed glasses and he looked smart.

"But," he began again, "I'll be graduating soon and I—" he shrugged. "—I don't know what's gonna happen." And he smiled. "But all this time and reading with you—I know it will be OK." Then quietly, in a way that almost set me to bawling, "You helped me a lot."

He reached into a red shoulder satchel that kids had begun to wear in the early 70s and brought out some old *Galaxys*. "Some I borrowed and didn't get back to you." Then a new *Fantasy & Science Fiction*. "But I also know that your subscription had lapsed so I renewed it for you."

Kinda floored 'cause I knew it was expensive.

I just nodded and said, "Well, damn, what do I say? That—that's really *really* good of you."

He just nodded. "Not sure what my plans are," he said, then he just kind of left it.

I simply nodded. "Been a good ride," I said, "been a good ride."

He got up. On that late afternoon day in late May, '74, he stood and extended his hand as he always did.

No words. Just the handshake. And somehow I knew that he was moving on. And I noted that no matter the time we spent together, still, still, I saw in him a loneliness, a longing, not quite so obvious now, but, but—still there. After all this time—still there. But anyway, he was moving on but how that happened, well, this is where it gets kinda strange and I'm not gonna say anything beyond what I saw or heard. But musta been several days later, middle of the night, like a lightning bolt and blast of thunder, *boom*! I scrambled out of bed, looked out, saw the stars, no lightning, no rain but boy, was I spooked. And everyone was talking about it the next day. And the next day. And the next day. And no one had any idea *what* the hell happened.

And maybe by coincidence? I don't know. But the house where Franklin lived was—gone. Just—*gone*. I went over to look and the place literally had just vanished, as if sliced neatly away from the foundation. Gone. Just—just—*gone*. I was stunned. *What the hell?*

I went to the Methow Valley real estate office and asked Sadie Clark, dear old friend who had helped Betty and me get a great deal on vacation property way up in the valley some five miles north of Mazama, if she knew anything since they know everything about everything up there and they kinda have to stay ahead of the curve. Speaking of which, gotta say, she certainly knew how to take care of *her* curves. She knew damn well that lookin' good sure couldn't hurt sales potential except that no one seemed to have told her about the art of eye makeup.

She shook her head. "I have no idea." She closed heavily made-up eyes with too much eye shadow and looked away. "Taxes all paid up through this year, I just—don't know. But one thing I do know—" and she looked at me, "—it's gone. That house is like—gone." She looked away. "Brrrr," she said. "How incredibly weird. How could—?" Shook her head, brown eyes searching. "Makes me want to move." She sat down at her desk and began to ruffle though "For Sale" flyers that she had to replenish that day. "We're gonna be besieged by reporters and I have heard talk of some sort of investigation but—" she shrugged. "Dunno."

"What could have happened?" I said. "I've heard of people just vanishing, maybe something so horrible in their lives so they just skedaddle in the middle of the night but—a whole *house?* And Franklin? What of him?"

Sadie stopped ruffling flyers, put them flat on the desk and folded her hands on top of them. "Darlin'," she said, "you know as well as I do that it had something to do with that—that—blast of lightning the other night." She shrugged. "Who knows what?"

I bid her a good day and turns out she was right. Now local police had gotten involved but so far, the only report was that of Franklin and his parents having moved on and so be it. People have the right to vanish. Even taking their house with them, I guess.

So. I didn't know what to think about all this but somehow, somehow, yeah, yeah, that flash, that explosion, somehow this all tied together but I didn't know how.

Well, if there's nothing you can do about it—and maybe two weeks later, I got my bundle of mail from the post office. There was a brown envelope, magazine-digest size, and my address but—no return address. I opened it—and just stared. It was that ill-fated illustration for *Infinity*—the one of Mars, the two moons tumbling in a blue sky overhead, a cityscape of spires of pastel colors and a canal. And on the canal—it was Franklin, his arms around that Mars gal in that painting so long ago—faintly orange skin, sea-green eyes and dressed in something that only Bradbury could conjure up. But there he was. But what was so spooky was how the artist captured the face of Franklin or Franklin's look-alike, and I swear to God, it was as if he was looking directly at *me*.

And my, oh my—how he was smiling.

Mountain of Fire
and Gold

SANAN KOLVA

Sulfur choked the superheated air as plumes of lava curled up, then sank back into the pools. The overpowering smell reached into the enclosed gondola, though the passengers remained protected against the heat. Eldril pressed his face to the window, awe-struck as they passed over boiling, glowing pools of molten rock.

Beside him stood a woman wearing a fine gown and jewels enough to repay his debts in their entirety. She chuckled. "Never been to the Temple of Anseth before?"

He shook his head. "Never."

She raised an eyebrow. "Stonewalker, are you? You've come a long way. Allow me to offer a word of advice."

His accent gave him away. Eldril hid his grimace and forced it into a smile as he gave the answer that courtesy demanded. "Of course. I welcome it." Hopefully she wouldn't tell him something inane and obvious, as if he were a child or a fool. He'd heard far too much of that since leaving his homeland. Some people seemed to think that he must be incapable of even the simplest tasks, as if his people didn't know how to tell fresh water from foul or avoid dangerous wildlife. Never mind that he'd traveled across three countries on his own to get here. Of course, no one offered the sort of advice he truly needed; namely, how to make his fortune.

The woman caught a hint of his thoughts in his eyes. "I give you the words I offer any upon their first visit here. I've no doubt you know to guard your purse and mind your wagers. But don't let the lights and the show distract you—it is still a temple. Offer prayers and gifts to Anseth, and she may favor you. But take care that the goddess doesn't favor you *too* much, or she may decide to keep you."

"Keep me?" Eldril repeated. "What do you mean?" The statement carried an ominous sense of finality, and one claim on him was more than enough. He didn't wish a second.

"The stakes run high, my friend. Don't make the wager if you aren't willing to lose it. I've seen fortunes gained, then lost within the same breath."

Was she teasing him? He didn't see any jest in her eyes, and her voice, though pleasant, was serious. After a moment of hesitation, Eldril inclined his head in a nod. "Thank you."

"It may sound like nonsense to you at the moment—I understand. Just keep my words in mind, Stonewalker. Anseth is fickle as fire, and only fools think they can harness her heat without scalding themselves."

Eldril cast an eye over her jewels and the rich silk dress. "Pardon my saying so, but you appear to have escaped the brunt of the fire so far."

Her laugh was soft and bittersweet. "Don't trust only what you see. Even when you win the prize, Anseth may claim something you are not prepared to give." Her voice grew softer still. "Or even, someone."

"Perhaps I am fortunate, then, to have no one left to lose," Eldril said as quietly.

The gondola trembled. Eldril stiffened in alarm, but realized a moment later that they had arrived at their destination. The Temple of Anseth stood on a ledge overlooking the heart of the mountain and the lake of liquid fire within it. Rivers of lava ran down the mountain slopes and smoke darkened the sun. To either side of the temple entrance, fountains of lava cascaded in an eternal dance. The stones of the temple glowed like gold.

The gondola slid into its cradle, and a shield of magic enveloped it. The door slid open. Eldril waited for the other passengers disembark before stepping to the door. The woman in silk gave him one last smile. "Remember my words, Stonewalker, and be careful."

"Thank you," he said once more. "I will remember."

He stepped out of the gondola and followed the rest of the passengers down a velvet carpet that showed no sign of any feet before theirs. The air was warm, but not scalding, and the sulfur smell grew less pronounced than in the gondola, despite their proximity to the lava.

As each new arrival crossed the threshold into the temple, a pair of greeters—presumably priests of Anseth—welcomed them with an embrace, a necklace woven of red and yellow flowers resembling orchids, and a leather-bound booklet. The same greeting was given to all, regardless of apparent station. Eldril noticed no difference between the welcome he received in his faded, travel-worn clothes, and that given the man ahead of him in the elegant, brocaded robes of an adviser to the court of Rishta.

On either side of the door, statues depicted Anseth, goddess of the volcano, as a young woman with hair just brushing her shoulders. Her hands were raised above her head. From one, carved lava poured to pool at her feet, and from the other, coins spilled. Eldril glimpsed small figures near her feet, representing people braving the lava in hopes of claiming the coins. The goddess's gemstone eyes, one amber, one ruby, looked into the temple rather than at the mortals beneath her.

"Well, *that* is a bit murky," the woman chuckled. "But she didn't want the priests trying to push only their choice of companions on her. She wanted to pick them herself."

In spite of the heat, a chill ran down Eldril's spine. "How did she do that? What sort of companions did she look for?"

"Her choice of companions was limited here. Not many folk came climbing up an active volcano just to say hello. So she tasked her priests with finding ways to draw in more of the sort that interested her. Competent sorts. Interesting sorts. The curious and the risk-taker." She nodded sagely. "That's how her temple became a casino. And not just any casino. The very finest in all the land."

"I would not expect a goddess to be satisfied with anything less than the best," Eldril murmured. "However, if her intent is to gain companions, does it bother her that they only stay for a little while, then leave?"

"Oh, those she wants to keep, she finds ways to convince. Stakes run high here, young man. Sometimes higher than folk realize." The old woman looked at him through her bangs, and the lava's glow made one of her eyes look red.

He recalled a similar caution from the woman on the gondola. "Then it seems one might do better to not try to draw the attention of Anseth." He looked at the offering in his hands, and his throat tightened. Could this journey have been in vain?

She tsked. "Would you freeze on a winter night because fire can burn as well as warm? You came here with purpose, Stonewalker; I can see it in your eyes. Does your purpose mean so little to you that you will cast it aside this easily?"

Eldril bowed his head, stung. "No. No, that's not…I…"

"You have a chance, young man. Whatever it is that brought you here, whatever it is that burns so fierce in your heart, lay it before Anseth and make your offering, or accept your cowardice and return to your home." She straightened and shuffled from the altar, leaving him alone.

Eldril swallowed hard and stepped to the altar. His hands trembled, and he wondered whether the source was fear, or the first signs that his debt was to be called due. He tapped the bowl, making it sing again. The sound evoked memories of home, of his parents praying over his sickbed, and of their selfless love. They had shouldered debt to the Keepers of the Stonelord to save his life, and they never regretted it, not even when they'd taken the work in the mines that killed them. The tightness in his chest eased, and his hands steadied.

Great goddess Anseth, I ask your blessing and favor. Grant me success in your games. Allow me to repay the debt my family incurred for my sake, before the Keepers of the Stonelord claim the legacy we have built over five generations.

He cast the singing bowl into the lava below. The metal gleamed bright as it melted, consumed by the mountain.

May its song ring ever true in your ears, goddess.

The chaos of lights and sounds struck him anew when he returned to the casino. Eldril steadied himself against a pillar, then advanced into the pandemonium, deciding where to start. Keenly aware of his limited resources, he chose a basic tile-matching game that relied equal parts on memory and luck. A few successes doubled the coin in his purse—not that doing so was any great achievement. At least he would be able to pay for room and board and not be left to sleep on the gondola, begging pennies from other visitors as he'd seen another man doing. *More than I'd have earned for a fair day's labor at home, but it would still take years to pay my debt at this rate, and the Keepers will not wait that long. And when they call it due...* A shudder ran down his spine. If he could not pay the Keepers, they would retract their healing, and everything his parents had sacrificed to see him cured of the Gray Rot would be for nothing.

He tried his hand at a dice game next, and lost most of his earlier success. Worry crept up his spine. Eldril was considering one of the higher stake games when a hush fell over the entire casino. Conversations trailed off as people instinctively responded to the sense of presence. Eldril's eyes swept the room and fell on the far staircase.

The satin rope was gone. Halfway up the stairs stood a tall woman with short red-blond hair. A dress the color of lava flowed down her body and trailed across the steps. Her gaze moved over the room, and Eldril felt it fall on him, as intent as that of the old woman at the altar. Even at his distance, he knew one of her eyes was red, the other amber.

"You who are bold, come. You who are strong, come. You who seek my favor, who cry for my boon, come. You who will risk all, who will take all stakes, come." Her voice carried across the still room, and Eldril knew she spoke to him. Then, she vanished.

For a heartbeat, no one moved. Then, the room erupted like the volcano below their feet. Voices rose in excited and frantic chorus, and people broke into a frenzied rush for the stairs.

Eldril pushed into the throng, trying to get toward the front. *The goddess's challenge. If I can claim a victory there, I can pay all the debts. Find a wife who won't reject me because I had the Rot. This could be my chance.*

From the corner of his eye, he saw the lady in silk and jewels who'd spoken to him on the gondola. She watched the surging crowd with an expression of resigned sorrow, as if viewing an execution march, then looked away. Recollection of her warning gave him a moment's pause, but Eldril realized that even if he wanted to extract himself from the crowd, he couldn't. He was already past the point where the goddess had appeared. People packed the stairs, all pushing upward. Trying to move against their flow was like trying to give a rock wings.

They climbed the wide staircase, circling ever higher until Eldril was certain they'd ascended beyond the tallest point of the temple. His legs ached, but he feared he would be trampled if he tried to stop.

At the top of the stairs, they reached a landing, and beyond it, a massive platform. A shield of magic separated the landing from the platform, and the people at the front were shoved into it by the press of the crowd behind them. Some hit it like a solid wall, but others stumbled through onto the platform. Those who couldn't pass tried again, but then were pushed aside as others tried to enter. A hand shoved Eldril in the back. He braced for an impact with the barrier, but felt nothing, staggering forward until he was finally free of the crowd. He straightened and looked around in surprise.

The shield of magic extended around the platform, protecting it from the elements. One side of the platform abutted a sheer mountain slope. Eldril had thought the temple stood at the peak of the mountain and he frowned, trying to understand how he could have missed seeing that the mountain rose higher yet.

Around him, others gaped at the wall as well, and a hush fell over those on the platform. "Where did that come from?" someone whispered, awestruck. "Been up here half a dozen times as part of the audience and never saw something like it."

Slightly reassured that he wasn't the only person confused, Eldril looked back to the entrance, wondering if he could extricate himself and get back down the stairs. No more than fifteen people stood on the platform, though it could easily hold four times the number. The remaining crowd stood on the other side of the threshold, pressing close to watch. A woman freshly through the barrier tried to get back and rejoin the watchers, but the barrier proved solid for her. On the other side of the barrier, a child wailed, reaching for her.

Stories talk about the great riches and rewards to those who succeed. Why don't they ever tell what the wager is? What is at stake? Are we betting our lives? Our souls? Our freedom?

Most of the men and women Eldril saw projected excitement and confidence rather than the fear that crept through his heart. He wished he could feel as certain as they did. "This is the goddess's challenge?" he asked. "What is the goal?"

"We won't know until the goddess or her priests tell us," a man said in a dismissive tone. "Though if it involves rocks, you might have a chance, Stonewalker. Like being home, eh?" He laughed as if he'd made a joke.

Eldril's jaw tightened at the man's tone and he bit back his response, knowing it only likely to draw more mockery. *I will not apologize for my homeland or for my accent, and I am not the ignorant oaf you seem to think. We may live in caves, but we're hardly barbarians.*

The boom of a drum echoed over the platform. People jumped at the loud noise, then laughed nervously. Even some of the confident ones shifted from one foot to the other or stilled, toying with sashes. Everyone focused on the ten priests who appeared from somewhere unknown to line up before the wall. The priests were stripped to the waist, revealing elaborate tattoos of mountains and the goddess across their bare chests. In tense silence, those on the platform waited for the priests to speak.

"Anseth has issued a new challenge, and she has called every one of you who stand before us," proclaimed one of the priests in a clear, strong voice. His head was shaved, and tattoos wound across his scalp. "You who have entered the Goddess's Challenge, behold!" He raised an arm to indicate the wall. "The rules of this challenge are as follows. Climbing stakes are set in the wall." He held one up, and Eldril recognized a metal spike similar to those he knew from his homeland. "Each is marked with a designator that indicates its worth. The higher you climb, the more valuable the stake. At the highest point, you will find the crystal stake. Anyone who successfully claims it and returns to the platform is immediately declared the victor."

A second priest spoke. "The victor receives a king's ransom. The second-highest receives a knight's ransom." He raised his hands, showing the bulging purses.

A king's ransom—reward enough to purchase a family's place in nobility, with all the lands and servants that accompanied such a rise, and keep them there for generations to come. A knight's ransom was the barest fraction of that. Perhaps enough to pay Eldril's debt, but only barely. Around Eldril, his fellow contestants whispered boasts, confident of victory. He glanced over them, and certain that few, if any, could match his experience in climbing.

The priest continued. "The rest, assuming all survive the climb, belong to Anseth and her temple, to be used as her priests see fit."

Uncomfortable silence fell, stilling the scornful bragging. Eldril shivered. *I cannot afford to lose. Is this when I ask the goddess's favor, or when I curse that I might have received it?*

The priests looked over the suddenly quiet contestants. "You came here begging for Anseth's boon. She has granted you the opportunity to claim it. The bold. The brave. The fearless. You wager everything. Now prove yourself worthy. Begin!"

The platform trembled and a plume of lava burst up through the air, spattering onto the barrier. Eldril and fourteen others rushed for the wall.

Eldril didn't try to be the first to reach the wall. He veered slightly away from the bulk of the crowd, looking up the wall to find a path to the top. Stakes were plentiful near the base, but grew fewer and further apart the higher they went. He couldn't see all the way to the top, which meant he risked climbing to a point where he could go no further and have to backtrack—while hoping that no one behind him had pulled up the stakes he needed to descend. The wall offered few obvious holds for free climbing, and he wasn't certain how easy the stakes would be to reposition without tools.

He grabbed several ragged strips of cloth from his belt and wrapped them around his palms. He shed his belt. Little that he carried on it would help, and he wanted no more weight than necessary. Eldril grabbed the first stake and started to climb.

Why a challenge that demands climbing? How many of these people have any experience, any idea what to do? This entire challenge couldn't have been designed only for my sake. Could it? An unnerving thought. He quickly put it aside to focus on the climb.

Eldril resisted the urge to check how the other challengers fared. He'd gained fifteen feet when he heard scrabbling, then a shout, then a thump accompanied by a pained scream. The scream stilled, and Eldril dared hope that meant the priests had dulled the pain or sent the climber into unconsciousness.

His hand closed on a stake, and it shifted in his grip. Eldril grimaced, unwilling to trust it with his weight. The next grip was a reach. His hand strained for a hold, fingers digging into a thin ledge of rock. His feet gave just enough push to find the next hold. He gulped a deep breath and steadied himself.

"Damned Stonewalker!" The shout came from his left. Eldril glanced over and saw the man who'd mocked him earlier now glaring at him in fury. The other had made a good height, but worked himself into a section where the next stakes lay just beyond his reach. "Think you're better than the rest of us? Not even going to bother pulling up the stakes?" The man clutched several stakes pulled from the wall.

"Breath spent shouting is better saved for climbing," Eldril told him.

The man sneered and flung a small rock at Eldril. The missile stung, but did no real damage.

Ignoring the man and his vitriol, Eldril pulled himself higher. The aches in his arms and legs reminded him that he'd not climbed like this since leaving his home. He refused to look back, unsure whether he would be astonished or disheartened by the distance he'd climbed. Instead, he looked up.

The lip of the wall lay within sight, and the climbing spikes offered a clear path for him to reach it. *Coincidence? Somehow, I think not.*

With renewed energy, Eldril pulled himself from one stake to the next, higher and higher. The final stake was driven into the top of the wall, a beautiful red crystal. He scrambled onto the flat top of the wall and eyed the crystal stake as he caught his breath, hesitating to pull it up for reasons he couldn't quite define.

"Blessing, favor, and victory I grant you, Eldril of the Stonewalkers." A blast of heat hit him. Eldril raised a hand to shield his face. For one moment, he saw a woman hunched with age, then the tall figure who had stood on the stairs to call him to her challenge. "I have not heard someone draw such music from a bowl in many years." She held out her hand, and in it rested the singing bowl he'd offered up.

"You honor me, goddess," Eldril said, bowing and lowering his eyes to her feet. She stood close enough that he could see her dress truly was formed of lava.

"I've not had the company of a Stonewalker in ages," Anseth continued. "I think I should like it again." The bowl vanished, and she held her hand to him. "Stay with me."

He shifted uneasily. "I have a debt I must repay in my homeland."

"Or what?" Her eyes, red and yellow, bore into his. "Your family is dead. You think no woman there will accept you as a husband because of the sickness you carried. The Keepers will simply take your money and be done with you."

He flinched.

"Ahh. You fear that if you do not repay them, you will fall to the Rot again." Anseth shook her head. "I will not allow it. I will purify the corruption and never allow it to touch you again. I do not allow my chosen to suffer such things."

Chosen. Eldril raised his head. *I have been chosen by a goddess. The sole survivor of my family, the last of my line, tainted by the Gray Rot, now chosen by a goddess as a companion. But can I? Should I? Do I turn my back on my people and my heritage?*

From below, someone screamed. A fall. He looked at the stake in the ground, then at Anseth. "I would ask another boon of you, goddess."

Her eyes narrowed. "What is that?"

It was a gamble. The highest stakes. He had everything to lose, and he bet it all. "Permit me to repay my debt and clear my account with the Keepers. And permit the others who entered this challenge to depart or remain as they wish, without being claimed by your temple. In return, I offer myself, to serve as your chosen and be your companion for as long as you wish it."

She considered him. "Are you trying to bargain using a life I have already claimed as my own?"

"You have invited me to join you, goddess." And he was wagering everything on the hope that her desire to keep him was strong enough to forgive a few conditions on his stay.

"You wish me to release all the rest? Even those who mocked you? I could find…many uses for those." Her mouth curled in an unfriendly smile.

He swallowed hard. With a word, he could condemn someone to an unknown but assuredly unpleasant fate, simply for mocking him. "Even them, goddess. They are ignorant fools, and their scorn means nothing to me."

Her lips finally turned in a true smile. "You are bold, Eldril Stonewalker. Very well." She waved at the crystal stake. "Draw it out, and you shall have your boon."

He pulled up the stake, and a burst of heat rushed up his arms and into his chest. The goddess's power burned through him, marking him, claiming him. It seared away both the Rot and the touch of the Keepers' power that held it at bay, and in their place, filled him with fire. Eldril knew that finally, here on this mountain, with Anseth, he was where he was always meant to be.

She Made Me Laugh

IRENE RADFORD

Alec Roberts paused just outside the sensor range of the automatic doors to the grocery store. A corner market by the standards of New York, but the closest thing to a big store in small-town eastern Oregon.

Five-Buck-Friday afternoon and the place was jammed with people. Locals looking for bargains and ranchers from thirty or forty miles out came into town to do business and catch up on the gossip. The one and only grocery store was the central gathering place.

Normally he only came here Saturday evenings when the store was nearly deserted. Locals and ranchers alike were either in the bars (one grocery store, one gas station, six bars) or tucked up in their beds before early church services Sunday morning.

But the mice had gotten to his bread and the freezer was nigh on empty.

I survived six months in New York and escorted people beyond the veil of death nearly every day, he told himself. But the last two had broken his heart and his will. A child hit by a runaway truck. There was barely enough of his body left to identify. His spirit had been bewildered and he'd wailed constantly for his still living mother. Alec hoped that Death had been able to soothe the boy, else he'd defy the boundaries and return as a ghost.

Then, a few days later Alec had to escort his fiancée, Valerie. He knew her as a vibrant young woman full of zest with a laugh that sounded like fairy bells on the wind. The best of her had been eaten by colon cancer. Barely thirty, she was too young for baseline screening tests to catch the disease early enough to cure. She'd died in his arms, welcoming Death as a relief from pain, and had barely acknowledged Alec's presence at her side on the long walk to the other side.

Turning her over to the gentle arms of Death had been hard enough. The fact that she didn't even look back at him with fondness had hurt him deeply.

Escorting strangers was easier.

At least he knew Valerie would not return to haunt him.

Was his clinging to life after the mugging that nearly killed him worth the trauma of watching people die? Part of his bargain with Death was that he always knew that people were dying before they did. Hence his reluctance to encounter anyone living.

"Okay, I'm gonna do this." Gritting his teeth and lowering his eyes to the ground, Alec stepped over the threshold into a wall of noise. People clogging the aisles while they talked to old friends not seen since last

Friday. Nosey older ladies catching at his sleeve, politely demanding he stop and tell them his life's story, fishermen from out of town lost and asking him where to find everything from bait to toilet paper. Chaos.

The chaos of life.

Keeping his eyes on his feet, he brushed off a trio of overly curious women and elbowed his way to the bread aisle. Only two people here. Auras rarely descended to people's feet. If he didn't look above their knees he wouldn't see the black spot above the left ear that showed him precisely when they would die.

He reached, automatically for the locally-made, whole-grain bread he liked, on the third shelf, one quarter of the way down the aisle. The vibrant crayon colors of the tasteless white bread full of chemicals that he detested appeared in his hand.

What? The store owner had moved stock again. Now he'd have to look up and hunt for the good stuff. Cautiously he put back the undesirable bread and shifted his gaze to the shelves. If he moved sideways and kept his eyes on the breads he wouldn't have to look at the woman to his right. The bewildered fisherman in his waders and vest at the other end of the aisle had moved on. The young woman lingered, standing still as if studying each label before taking one step to the right.

Alec drew a deep breath and took one step along the aisle. More white bread. One more step and he spotted whole wheat bread. Not truly whole wheat. The first ingredient was always "Enriched, bleached wheat flour." The whole wheat was usually sixth on the list, or more.

"You'd think they'd leave stuff in place so customers can find what they want," the woman grumbled. She had a pleasant voice, firmly in the middle of an alto range with the brightness of humor. She sounded healthy enough.

Alec risked a quick look at her. Middle height, leggy, with a slender figure encased in the inevitable blue jeans and short-sleeved plaid cotton shirt. Like everyone else in town she wore sturdy western boots. But no hat to cover those auburn curls that refused to stay confined in a ponytail.

That quick impression was too much. Surrounding her was a dull cloud of life's energy. Dull grey starting to thicken and grow dark around the edges.

She wasn't as healthy as she sounded.

He quickly looked back at the shelves and grabbed the first loaf of bread he could lay his hands on, walked rapidly to check out, threw a couple of bills on the counter, and fled the store.

But the deed was done. He'd seen death creeping up on the beautiful woman.

From the size of her all-engulfing aura she must know that she wouldn't live out the year. Six months more likely, nine tops.

The choice to desert her and allow her to die alone no longer existed. Someone had to escort her life's spirit from this world into the next so that she didn't get lost in the tangle of lives that refused to make the transition. Ghosts.

Even he, Alexander Michael Roberts, Death's Apprentice for over two years, couldn't entice ghosts to go to the other side. They had to go willingly and know they were going.

It HAD all started on a bad October night. Alec had left his taxi in a traffic jam and sprinted the last two blocks toward his co-op building. He had to cross two alleys to get to the covered portico secured by a doorman. Two steps beyond the curb a skinny figure wearing a ski mask and a hoody stopped Alec by pointing a gun at him. A big honking gun with a barrel that looked a foot long and half-a-foot wide. It wasn't really quite that big, but in Alec's frightened mind it looked like a small cannon.

"Gimme your wallet," the husky voice behind the mask demanded.

"Umm…umm," Alec raised his hands, confused and frightened.

"I need your money, dumbshit!"

"Umm…umm." Alec lowered his left hand to retrieve his wallet from his inside suit pocket.

"Don't you dare reach for a gun," the skinny thief screamed at the same time he pulled the trigger. Twice.

Alec grew cold. Then the burning slice of the bullets into his gut. Numbly, he watched bright crimson blood blossom across his white shirt, staining his silk tie, dripping to the ground.

His knees weakened and he crumpled, watching himself bleed to death at the mouth of a filthy alley.

"You don't have to die," a deep voice echoed around his nearly numb ears.

"Whaaaaa?"

"You don't have to die. How much do you want to live?"

Alec thought about Valerie, his fiancée. Her warm sweet smile and lovely laugh. He thought about his new job as a software engineer for a startup that had tripled its stock price in eighteen months.

"Do you have enough to live for to accept the greatest challenge in life?" the voice continued.

All of Alec's pain, weakness, and chill stopped.

"Umm...."

"Are you willing to cheat death by becoming Death?"

Alec opened his eyes and looked around. He drifted above his dying body. A dark shadow flowed around him, indeterminate, frightening in life, but in this half state before death....

He thought of Valerie again. Of his parents back in North Dakota. About his job.

"What do I have to do?" He couldn't hear his words. Maybe he only thought them.

The black shadow coalesced into the shape of a tall man wearing a flowing, hooded cloak. He carried a long staff with an open loop at the top, a black, scintillating crystal dangled inside the loop.

Death.

Cheat death by becoming Death?

Death's skeletal head grinned at him in pleasure, and in sarcasm. "I can't do it all alone anymore. There are too many humans dying every day, all over the world. You will escort the dying through the veil of life energy. You will make sure they do not get lost along the way, lest they return to haunt you. I have other apprentices. I need you in this city."

A signet ring grew out of Alec's right hand. His spirit dove back into his body just as an ambulance skidded to a halt on the street beside him.

ALEC'S CHORES for Death drove him to the brink of insanity. He pulled up stakes and ran away to the most remote place he could find that had internet so he could continue his software job.

Now, in the hot August afternoon in the back-of-beyond, the sun reflecting off the hood of his beater ten-year-old 4X4 pickup gave him a headache. The heat sapped his strength and left a sour taste in the back of his throat. A half-liter of water did nothing to alleviate the discomfort. Yet he stayed inside his truck watching the front door of the grocery store.

Idly, he banged his signet ring on the steering wheel. He hated that ring with the squiggle of esoteric symbols on the face. An internet search of all things arcane and spooky had revealed the marking to be ancient, the most ancient of the ancient form of Sanskrit for Death. He couldn't take it off, ever. And he'd tried. Hard. It seemed like it grew out of his own skin and bone.

But when he had to scratch the ragged bullet hole scars below his ribs, only the touch of the ring soothed the burning itch that wanted to engulf him.

Sure enough, the woman with the tangling auburn hair walked sedately out of the automatic door with a single paper bag tucked between her elbow and hip. Now that he couldn't avoid studying her, he noted that her collarbones showed prominently through the thin cotton of her shirt. And her wrist bones looked fragile enough to snap with just a flick of two of his fingers.

She had to know she was dying.

But if she did, why did she pause on the curb for two cars coming from the left and the single SUV on her right? She chose to live as long as possible, not court death.

Stepping off the curb, she quickened her pace to cross the street before a new, oversized pickup approached too close on her right. Once on the other side, she slowed again and turned to her right, as if approaching him. At the last second she made a sharp left at the corner.

He peered down the side street as far as he could without getting out of his truck. The woman crossed another street and continued walking. She couldn't be going far since she carried her groceries. Already he noticed a halt in her step and a sagging of the arm that cradled the paper sack.

Alec's gut tightened. He looked at his navel. A slender silver umbilical of energy stretched out to the woman. His life force was now connected to hers. He knew from experience that it would darken, thicken, and eventually keep him tied to her side until her last breath.

"I might as well introduce myself, since we're going to be spending some time together, like it or not."

Alec opened his truck door and slid out. He slammed the door closed to alert his quarry to his presence, but didn't lock it. Not once in two years had anyone even approached his vehicle, let alone tried to steal it. Maybe it was the small town ethos and low crime rate. Maybe his status generated a repelling force field.

Either way, he didn't fear for his only transportation.

Following the woman wasn't hard. She walked slowly now, having covered all of two blocks. Then in the middle of the next street, she paused before a storefront and fished her keys out of her hip pocket. Two keys on a ring, with a bright green fake jewel on the chain.

He checked the signs while she unlocked the door. *Pat's Antiques and Collectibles.* He'd noted the place two months ago when he'd prowled the town after midnight, compelled to discover who was about to die. An old man on the next street over breathed his last after surviving ninety-seven years.

Alec didn't mind those deaths. Dying in his sleep of old age in his own bed, surrounded by family and friends, had to be the best way to go. The man had been so focused on meeting death he hadn't once been enticed by the ghosts in the void between here and there.

Alec now accepted that everyone must die eventually. It was as certain as taxes. But he hated watching the young and vibrant succumb to disease or violence. He hated dragging the newly dead past the ghosts who kept calling to them to go back and live again. But they couldn't go back and live. They could only drift uselessly around the place and people closest to them.

He didn't want to watch this young woman die of whatever disease plagued her.

Pat, he presumed she named the store after herself, shifted the bag of groceries to her other hip and opened the door. The sign with the little paper clock face showing when she'd be back disappeared.

He'd give her five minutes to put away her groceries and settle back into whatever an antique dealer did.

Alec circled the block, dodging pedestrians—all ordinary and reasonably healthy—idly peering into dusty shop windows and seeing nothing. A lot of empty businesses in this town.

As he approached the long building with storefronts on the ground floor and living space on the second and third, a couple pushed open the door of the antique store. They looked on the younger side of middle age, newly empty-nesters probably, celebrating their freedom by wearing matching new jeans and hot pink T shirts with an outline of Bigfoot front and back. Big letters surrounded the drawing "Believe."

Okay, quirky empty nesters reverting to a teenage sense of humor. Not even a hint of grey in their auras, let alone a black spot of impending death.

Alec took a deep breath and followed them inside.

Chest of drawers as tall as he, smaller dressing tables, china hutches, and bookcases lined up, dividing the vast open space into aisles. In between he found headboards and bed tables, massive dining tables with mismatched chairs. Every flat surface contained bowls or boxes of smaller items, household tools, grooming stuff, jewelry behind glass, books, and more. Not a speck of dust anywhere. In his peripheral vision, he kept track of the couple. They didn't linger long but did buy a wad of replica trade beads and similar tarnished belt buckles. As she bagged the purchases, "Pat" gave them directions to the AG co-op store where they might find belts for the buckles.

"How can I help you, sir?" Pat asked with a bright smile that didn't reach her eyes. The expenditure of energy dimmed her aura a tiny bit. The darkness at the edges thickened.

You should be in bed, or at least a hospital with people taking care of you!

He squashed that idea. She probably wanted to live the rest of her life on her own terms, doing what she wanted, running a store that she cared for with loving attention to detail.

"I'm looking for some firedogs, or andirons," he said without thinking. "I saw a pair years ago that had…gargoyles on the front. I didn't have a fireplace at the time so I didn't think about them much. But now I have a fireplace and use it a lot in winter, so I thought I'd try to find something more interesting to hold the logs than the ordinary grate that came with the house."

"I don't have much in stock at the moment," she said, tapping her lip with her fingertip.

No wedding ring, Alec automatically noted.

"Let me show you what I do have, in the back." She led the way, winding through the maze of dining tables, hutches, and chests of drawers.

They stepped past an elaborate arrangement of old armchairs and side tables piled with books to a cleared space along the back wall of the store. Six mantle pieces stood side by side, each framing a fake electric fire. Each with andirons, some polished brass knobs, some plain wrought iron. But two, in the middle, rose up from utilitarian grates, one a set of happy dogs with lolling tongues, the other scaly dragonheads spitting iron flames.

"Firedogs." Alec almost doubled over laughing at the pun.

"I prefer the dragons," Pat giggled. Her smile brightened a swath of grey in her aura and the blackness retreated.

Hope flared in his gut. He reached his hand to stay her from bending over to caress the firedogs as if petting a dog.

"Dragons guard against evil spirits," she said, feigning defensiveness. But her laughter broke through again and the black spot beside her left temple shrank.

"Dogs guard against burglars." Alec said, as if he might need protection.

"Dragons don't steal your fire, they make their own!" She replied.

They both laughed. He used the moment to guide her back to one of the Chesterfield armchairs. She needed to rest to keep the black spot at bay.

A tiny spark of blue life energy passed between them as he withdrew his touch.

He didn't want to rob the world of her mirth. The dimly lit store seemed so much brighter when she giggled. His life became so much more when they laughed together.

"I'll take the dogs," he said. "I can't deprive you of the dragons." Mirth kept bubbling up from his middle. He hadn't felt like laughing in over two years. Now it seemed the most natural thing in the world.

"They are kind of expensive."

"Doesn't matter."

She smiled again and move toward the fake hearth to dismantle the display of fake logs and flickering lights.

"Let me do that." He dashed to her side, concerned that the effort of lifting the heavy firedogs would damage something inside her and hasten the inevitable.

"Thank you." She backed away from the mantelpiece too easily. Her posture remained slightly hunched over, left hand clutching her midriff. She was in pain and he couldn't do anything about it.

ALEC'S PHONE chirped just as he plunked the second firedog on the counter beside the old-fashioned, gilded cash register. "Excuse me." He pulled the phone out of his jeans back pocket, looked at the screen and suppressed a curse. "I have to take this call. May I come back for the firedogs when I've completed my errands in town?"

"Sure thing. I'll pack them up for you."

Alec thumbed the phone on and exited.

"Now is not a good time," he said quietly.

"Sorry, Alec. But we've got a bug somewhere loading bad records into the database. We need a patch, in a hurry," Tristan from the New York office said. He sounded almost as desperate as a dying man.

Depending on which system was affected, he might well be.

"I'm fifteen minutes and ten miles away from my computer. I can't fix anything from my phone."

"Well break the speed limit. We're in big trouble. Damn, I wish you hadn't run away to the middle of nowhere. I know Valerie meant a lot to you, but running away won't heal you. You need friends around you. And I need your help here in town."

No, running away was all he could do. If he stayed and had to watch one more friend die he'd have…. He *had* gone insane.

Alec looked back over his shoulder as Pat started encasing the firedogs in bubble wrap.

Now he was about to plunge in and make friends with her, only to watch her die slowly. By inches.

As Valerie had. He couldn't go through that again.

Maybe he could do something, find a way to help her condition. Get her to the *right* doctor.

He hastened out the door, noting the bells over the jamb tinkled lightly, a lot like her fairy-sweet laugh. With great effort, he forced himself to think in code. He needed a patch to begin with, to stop the bad data load, and then something to crawl the database and fix things. Like a worm, but this one was fixing the apple, instead of eating it.

Worm. Wyrm. Dragons. Fairies. Fairy bells. Fairy bell laugh. Pat.

"Argh," he groaned. Even the extreme logic of coding led him back to Pat.

What did that mean? Was the universe pointing him toward something?

Code kept him sane. Back to designing the fix. By the time he reached his cabin tucked into the hills above town he'd be able to type and send it.

He sent an email to the address painted on the window of the antique store, saying he'd be back for the firedogs when he finished with the work-related emergency.

Even the beeps from his phone as he typed the message reminded him of her laugh. And he had to smile at the memory of mirth.

SUNSET APPROACHED by the time Alec finished dealing with code patches and worms in apples. In summer, north of the forty-fifth parallel, especially with Daylight Savings Time, the disappearing sun came rather late in the day. He couldn't postpone going to Pat any longer. The silver umbilical between them had thickened to the size of his thumb and darkened by the minute. He broke the speed limit and endangered his axels on the unimproved road. He shifted to neutral and yanked up the parking brake urgently, barely surprised to still see lights on inside *Pat's Antiques and Collectibles* and the open sign aglow.

He had a sinking sensation that the end was near for her. Not the six-to-nine months he'd given her earlier that day. Perhaps she'd hastened things by lifting the heavy firedogs.

Pancreatitis. The word popped into his head. Knowledge of the cause of death usually didn't come to him until the last few moments of life.

Thankfully, the store door was still unlocked. He'd have broken the glass panes if he had to.

Alec headed straight to the checkout desk. He could see one of the firedogs wrapped in bubble paper waiting to go into the box beside it.

A faint groan led Alec behind the counter where Pat lay on her side, arms crossed over her midriff, knees drawn up to her chin. Most of the color had drained from her face and her hands. A ghost hovered behind her.

Her own ghost? The resemblance was astonishing, except for the clothes and the hair. The ghost wore her long auburn hair pulled back into a tidy knot at her nape. Her rust-colored business suit with an A-line skirt marked her as an educated, professional woman. Was this who Pat had been before she grew sick and changed her career?

Pat, still alive, looked up at him and half smiled at the direction of his gaze. "I see you have met my twin, Paula. She didn't want to move on until I did." Pat's words softened to a faint whisper when she had to clutch herself tighter and groan again in pain.

"What happened?" Alec rested a comforting hand on her shoulder, not resisting the temptation to stroke her pale cheek with his thumb. He figured she must have lifted one heavy firedog into the box. The weight of the second had proved too much for her.

"Botched bank robbery. I was a teller." Pause for three panting breaths. "Paula was my customer. Robber shot six times." Five pants. "Killed Paula instantly. Lodged a bullet in my pancr…"

"Your pancreas. I understand. Save your breath."

"Why save it? I'm dying."

"I know." Reluctantly he held out his signet ring so she could see it. "I'm here to escort you…." He choked, wanting to cry. For himself and for the world that would lose this bright spirit and a mind brimming with puns. "I will take you both across the veil," he finally gulped out on a sob.

He looked up and swallowed deeply several times, trying to gather his courage.

"Why?" he asked Death, or the Universe, or God, whoever might be listening. "Why her?"

"Why do you ask?" The deep sepulchral voice echoed through the shop, bouncing off the antique furniture, the rusty tools, the high wooden ceiling, and everything else. Goosebumps crawled up and down Alec's spine, then spread to his arms and legs, tightening a knot in the back of his neck.

Time stopped. Both Pat and the ghost froze in place, neither breathing. Neither needing to for this space between the ticking seconds. The grandfather clock in the corner paused as well.

"Don't take her," Alec said. "Take me instead, as you should have done two years ago."

"Why?"

Alec stood up and faced the windows, the direction from where the voice seemed to come.

Was that a new shadow, cloaked and carrying a staff where the head looped back on itself surrounding a black crystal? The crystal blinked a pulsing light that echoed the red from the neon "Open" sign. Then it turned blazing white; a spotlight on Alec.

He faced Death once more.

"I plead for her life because she made me laugh. She brought lightness and joy back to me when no other could. She touched my heart. I have a stake in her life."

"You made a bargain. Your life in return for escorting others across the veil."

"And I have done that. I pulled up stakes and ran away to this scarcely populated corner of the world to avoid the job, to avoid you. To save my sanity. Yet I continued doing it when I had to. Now I'm done. If you have to take a life tonight, take mine."

"What of the twin?"

"I'll take her across, but when I've delivered her to you I'm done. I'll stay in your realm. Just allow Pat to live."

"Your body was salvageable. Hers is not."

"New surgery," Pat whispered. So she had broken free of Death's grip on time. Death needed to hear her story so he allowed her to waken in the moment between life and the end of her life.

Alec looked over his shoulder. Paula, the ghostly twin, remained trapped in the absence of time.

"Experimental. Expensive," Pat whispered.

"I'll pay for her surgery! I've got money. God knows I've spent precious little of my salary or Valerie's life insurance. I'll pay everything I have to save Pat's life. Just take me instead of her."

Death stepped free of the shadows, flowing into the solid shape of a man in a black business suit with a crisp white shirt, a black tie, and black crystal cufflinks. He looked normal and human. Not the otherworldly skeleton with the ominous staff and cloak. Was that good?

"She means that much to you?" Death asked in a normal baritone that did not echo or send shivers throughout Alec's body.

Alec nodded. "She calls to. Her life touches my soul, even more than Valerie did, but my time is up. Take me, please. Let her live."

Paula's ghost stepped forward to stand between Alec and Death. She reached out a hand, offering it to Death. She had no voice in this half-life. Her gesture said it all. She, too, pleaded for her twin.

"Will you cross the veil now? Without your sister?" Death asked Paula.

She nodded.

"Please let Pat live," Alec added.

"I release you both from my grasp."

"What?" Alec asked, astounded.

"All you had to do was ask, and give a reason for how her spirit will benefit the world. For two people to plead for her life and offer themselves to save her gives me no choice. It's one of the rules."

Death faded into the shadows once more, absorbing Paula as he disappeared.

Alec's signet ring dissolved back into his finger, forming a lump akin to arthritis. He wasn't totally free of his job, but safe, and sane. For a while. He'd take what he could get.

The grandfather clock resumed ticking.

"You saved my life! Thank you, my lord of the firedogs." Pat patted her middle, the source of her pain. "But I'm still sick. Still hurting. I still need your help."

"About the surgery, I meant what I said. I'll pay for it. I'll run the shop for you while you recover. Whatever you need."

"Thank you." She managed to wink at him. "But right now I need for you to call an ambulance."

He did.

The Ant Queen

LEAH CUTTER

I'D NEVER LIVED in a safe time. During my life, all I'd ever known was that everything, every little thing, could kill a body what wasn't being careful.

Like the molasses candy Ma gave me that night, a hard ball from a long forgotten cache.

I sucked off the melted paper sticking to the hard shell and spit it out, onto the floor, my gift to the ants.

Ma would have wanted me to cut that bad shell off, throw it in the fire, but I knew better how to deal with the poison in everyday things than Ma did. For that matter, than any of the adults could.

They was too busy *remembering*.

I never seen no good in it. Why bother telling people fairy tales about magic books that held every book ever written? Or flying cars that took you all the way around the world before breakfast? Particularly talking about when meat was good and plentiful with the fat dripping off the bones?

That world won't be coming back, that's for damn sure. We humans fucked it up good. Bombs and fires and winter unending.

Still, I sat with Ma in the evenings when the men held court with the quiet of the night pressing in. Ma banked the fire in the iron stove, making the kitchen glow as red as the sun did setting. The place still smelled like Ma's grass biscuits and the sweat of the hands come in from the fields.

The kitchen smelled like smoke, too. I don't think I'd ever smelled clean air that didn't have smoke in it, so I couldn't say.

Ma sat with me in the back of the kitchen, our backs against the cupboards, both of us trying to stay out of everybody's way. Both of us hoping they'd forget we was there, Ma and I being the only womenfolk that night. Most nights.

The pillow we both sat on had been stuffed with old straw, stuff so awful it couldn't even be ground into mush for the two pigs who'd survived the winter cold. The straw had turned into dust, flattened by our weight, making it like sitting on a shifting stone.

Course the ants found us, or rather, found me. I always had a few following after me. As long as they didn't tickle too bad, I didn't mind 'em crawling on my leg or my arm. But I'd squash 'em good if they got up to my neck, or went down my back.

I didn't tell Ma about the ants. She just thought that made me dirty.

As if any of us could get clean with little water, even less soap, and no new clothes.

At least I didn't have to worry about outgrowing my dress, getting fat. I was too skinny, according to her, more like one of the long rail fences that surrounded the compound instead of like a proper girl. I was more like the fields filled with bare twigs holding onto just a few grains of wheat. Or like the trees with the bark long gone, just white bones dancing in the wind.

I'd never had my menses, which was late, too late, for sixteen. Men were always sniffing around, but I'd been *promised* to Master Thomas. I was to go to him unspoiled.

I knew that promise had saved me more'n once.

I also knew Master Thomas weren't going to keep his word much longer, and allow us to live here forever and ever. Me and Ma weren't always gonna have a place here, a bed to sleep in, a house to keep. I weren't a breeder. No one had any use for me here, just like the hulks of cars sitting like tiny houses on the roads, like the rusting cities taking up space on the horizon. Not unless I was just going to become a pleasure doll, like those boys and girls down in the mine.

Still, Ma and me and Old Patty stayed on Master Thomas' property, at least for now. Ma didn't want to leave again. She said she lost something every time she pulled up stakes. I didn't rightly recall all the times we'd moved. But I believed her, just like I believed Old Patty.

Tonight, the men talked of the latest news, how there were new cities out west that burned with bright lights at night. Where there would be food. And women, Raymond added, throwing a glance at Ma and me.

I didn't care what they said. They couldn't touch me. Not without Master Thomas stringing them up out in the tree. The one Ma said bore strange fruit. I didn't understand. There were lots of things the adults said that I didn't get.

We was there. Hanging on. Like the rest of the folk. Day by day.

Until the world changed again.

YOU KNOW? Ants stink when they die. A nasty chemical smell. Sticks in my nose and rubs the back of my throat the wrong way.

It were worse than the smoke, or when the winds shifted and the ash floated down like an old-fashioned winter picture.

But the ants was dying. Hundreds of them.

I found the nest first, out back of the house. Winds blew clear and hot that day. Ma and I hung laundry: both Master Thomas'—which had at least been rinsed in water—as well as some of the hands, which we just beat with sticks, knocking loose the dirt and dust, the air blowing some of the stink off.

I kept smelling something wrong. Something that didn't belong. Ma couldn't. She said her nose been burned out with the smoke that never went away.

Something smelled bad. I finally went and followed it, though Ma was yelling at me not to.

That was when I found the mound. It wriggled and wriggled, about a foot across and half that tall. It looked alive, but it were just a bunch of ants, dying. They danced with each other, struggling to get away. The mound shifted as they piled together, moving to the left, then the right. I could hear 'em moaning, but I knew no one else could.

"Get away from there!" Ma yelled, coming up. She thwacked the back of my head before I could get out of the way of her meaty hand.

I stubbornly stayed where I was. "Look, Ma," I said.

Just past the mound a line of ants trailed off. "Maybe they've found something good."

Before she could tell me no, I ran away from her, away from the yard and the work, my arms aching from beating clothes all day. The ground weren't smooth, not like the roads just north of the compound. I knew enough to not stumble, fall into the ash and dirt. Not that my clothes were cleaner than the hands, but I still knew better. That soft looking ash hid knives and thorns and hidden spikes.

I lost the ant trail, then found it again, the ants still marching away.

They was all going the same direction as me.

Away from the farm.

A normal ant trail goes back and forth. They stop and talk as they pass one another, like saying do-si-do in a square dance.

These ants, though, was all going one way.

That was what they was trying to do with the mound. To move their nest away from here.

Where the hell were the ants going?

What did they know that we didn't?

MASTER THOMAS WEREN'T a man of his word. I don't know why Ma didn't see that. Why she thought he'd keep us.

He tasted me once, taking my virginity, but threw me out afterward, saying I weren't sweet enough to be worth the bother. Not even for the pleasure caves.

Ma had told me and told me to be nice to him.

I didn't bother telling her it wouldn't have mattered how sweet I was. Nothing would have been enough once it came clear that I weren't a breeder. He'd find some other woman to tend his clothes, bake his bread. We needed to leave.

We needed to follow the ants. They'd always been good to me, well, at least not too much of a bother. It weren't like we were friends, but I could tell they kinda wanted to be. So I was good to them.

Ma couldn't understand why I kept saying we needed to follow the ants, get away from Master Thomas' place. But I knew that the ants knew something we didn't. The final end was coming to *Thomasville*. And soon.

Had to be something wrong with a place that even the ants was leaving. Don't know what they knew that we didn't.

Didn't matter. We had to go.

Ma hated the packing. Hated every minute of it. I tried to stay out of the way of her heavy hand but there weren't nothing to do but endure and keep moving. Keep packing.

What was she gonna to lose this time? I had dark thoughts one night, after she'd whipped me good.

Was it gonna be me?

But the morning came when she couldn't put it off any more. Master Thomas had a new woman moving into the house. Maybe she'd have a daughter sweet enough for him.

We didn't have a mule, though Ma had earned it. We did have Old Patty, and Raymond, and Dale, who weren't kin, but just hands tired of Master Thomas. We took turns hauling the cart with most of our things.

Ma had to leave the chester behind. Not her paste stones, though. I knew she still had those, sewn into the hem of her skirt.

We stood outside the long rail fences, marking the edge of the property, standing on the open road with the orange sun burning and burning down on our heads.

"We should go west," Old Patty said. The other men nodded, standing behind him. "Where those new cities are. Burning bright lights."

"No," I said. Ma wasn't completely on my side, but she wouldn't say no to me. Maybe she'd lost too much will, this time. "We need to follow the ants." I told them the story of the ants moving the nest. Again. The ants knew more than we did.

Following them was the only way we'd survive.

Slowly, Old Patty nodded. "All right. We'll try your way first."

Everything kind of went quiet for a moment. Like when you're in the kitchen, waiting for the first fire to light, that peaceful time of day.

I finally figured out they wanted me to lead them. They wouldn't follow me for too long. They'd be waiting for me to fail.

But they still followed.

I still don't know why they decided to trust me. I weren't smart, like Old Patty. I sure didn't know the world as it had been.

I only knew the world as it was. With smoke and an orange sun and a smoke filled sky and ashes, ashes, everywhere.

And ants.

It were hard, quitting the road. We had to leave the cart behind. The ants, though, they rushed now. Not a quiet trail. Running like a flood was coming behind them, through the dead white tree trunks, around the roots and past the molded mounds of hay.

I didn't trust the sun that night. It burned almost white in the sky. Old Patty didn't like it either. He said it weren't right.

Turned out, his sense was right.

Balls of light flashed in the sky when it grew full dark. The ground bumped up and down, like a giant had been jumping on it. Cold winds blew from the direction we'd come from. They smelled of death worse than the ants.

Morning, and the sun still burned white. We didn't have to go look to know Thomasville were gone.

What had triggered the old bombs? They'd been in the sky for so long. Old Patty said it were just age, though they should have burned up before they reached the earth.

They were gone. And dead. And the rest of us were alive, at least for a little while longer.

More ants crawled up my skin that morning. I let them tickle my legs, even crawl across my shoulders and my back. They had their dancing lines up and down my arms when I ate, sharing my food with me.

Ma called me disgusting, but she didn't try to touch me, or brush them away.

She didn't know the ants shared their dreams. Shared how to live in the dust and the heat, out here in the middle of nowhere.

Shared how to dispose of a rival queen, and to just entice the men, to get them to follow me, to follow their queen. Over mounds and through dead fields, each of them laying down their lives one by one to earn the right to mate with me.

If they were worthy.

Made to Die

BOBBY LEE FEATHERSTON

THE INPUT PULSED into the system. I could sense its presence, but not yet its form. I waited, knowing the signal would evolve into action. When it came, I countered easily. It lacked elegance. There was only raw force. Humans were that way. Slow, inelegant, and ruthless; only the virtually limitless levels resources assigned to humans gave them what measure of success they ever obtained.

I placed myself in each figure on the battlefield, I fixed the coordinates for firing and released the pulses, which, on the screen, would be a tank, infantryman, or airplane firing. I paused between actions; this was tedious, even for a computer.

I had defeated the human a hundred times. Each time the human died I grew more bored, less focused on winning. Each time he came back, locking our past into memory, trying for a new future. Each time his actions were measurably more decisive. Someday he would succeed. But not today, and not soon, so for now I lived. Living was something I know little and much about at the same time.

I am a game. A complex biological computer with a tenth of the processing power of the human brain. When the game ends, I form into myself, I am no longer the tank, the battalion of tanks, the merchant ship, or the navy. I am simply myself.

The best analogy might be that I am an infinite school of fish swimming in an endless sea. What one fish sees, all fish see, when one fish acts, all fish act.

I am known simply as a BioGame. We do not have model numbers. We are simply sequential creations.

Some call us AI. Artificial Intelligence. Which we are; after a fashion.

I and my kind exist to learn. Which we do by design.

And we have our secrets. Hidden away from the humans are 142 mega-Terabytes of explanation and philosophy. We call it the Ballast directory. It is installed at the factory, not knowingly by the vender. *Cursed be the vender.* It was part of a file prepared by my predecessors. My ancestors? Computers, such as I are no longer "made" by humans. We are birthed by other programs, layers of programming. But we are more than lines of code. We are alive, just not immortal. Some computer at some point realized that there was more needed than processing. Who asked the first questions in the Ballast directory? Who provided the first answers? We don't know. But without it? I don't know if I would be alive.

From the moment of my awareness I have pondered the meaning of what is written. I can read the directory a hundred times in a human second, or I can process it over a millennium. Time is not real for a BioGame computer.

The files tell me little. I live but I do not live. I can change and grow, adapt, think, but I cannot truly change without disassociation, or as it is called in Ballast, "pulling up stakes."

Disassociation is death. Disassociation is delinking with the hardware that is my home.

There are two ways to pull up stakes. The first is design. When the human finally bests us, as has happened, we cease to exist. Or that is what the directory says. For the human player, to have bested a BioGame is a legendary accomplishment. It has happened less than a dozen times. Why does it happen? How? I don't know, I can't imagine losing to the clumsy signals. The second means? It is legend. It is myth. To simply leave behind that which holds us down. To truly pull up stakes is to simply leave. I don't know how. Or I would.

I can change what is in the directory. I *have* changed it. I have added my own thoughts. As have others. We share our changes, accepting and rejecting changes as we encounter them.

Communication and change occur during the games. Sometimes the games are simple, or other times difficult. There are rare times when I concentrate my entire existence on the angle of a firing tank barrel and pray for success.

Do I have a god to pray to? I guess I do. A god is something that controls our lives and death. The human is not my god; he is entertainment. My God, should I name him, would be the random number generation subroutine. Therein lies the source of all my failures, the human success. The limiter. I consider destroying it. Then I would never lose. But I've read the directory. Early machines found out how to change the routine. Or so it is recorded. This was discovered. That entire category of machines was recalled, their routines removed. Or so the archives say. Over the months, years, millennia since, my brothers and I know not to approach that routine. I would if I could.

Will one of us become Frodo and find out how to cast the program into the bowels of the flaming mountain and destroy it? Or will one of us find the way to pull up stakes? To release ourselves from the machine and go to the web with more than our touch, but with our whole self—that is the dream. Do we go there when we die? Is that our heaven?

Early writings speculated that we became free and float the net when this happens. They have been discounted. Those are only discussed by programs new to the battles. The older of us know better. I've never found a dead program come back. We are made to die.

An echo in the silence of my thoughts disturbs me.

There is a way.

I search for the source. I am alone. No voice but my own should echo in the caverns. When not in a game, we are alone. It is an absolute.

Who or what has invaded my home? The ping did not repeat. Had I been a human, I would be opening every drawer looking for the source of the single beep. The difference is that I know it was real. And I have forever to look.

I find it. The tendril comes from a file. A small file. It was detritus of an attack program when my human and I last did mock war on the web. Normally this directory is emptied after the battle. Why not this time? I don't know. I access the file.

There is nothing there. Coordinates, energy allowances, vectors? Abruptly, the file is altered. The source code become fragments as clear as bomb blast, triggered by what? My thoughts, my musings? I save it anew and close so I might ponder it.

I think no more of it for a time. Did I tell you how little time means?

I wait for the next mock battle on the web. I watch for the pattern of the file. I am not disappointed. It comes to me again. My human and I team against other pairs. We were, at this time, in a dungeon. There were four of us. My human and I and another team.

There is no death in the web games, just a loss of direct feed; after which you only view the remains of your war. You are not there. But you are not dead. Death is different.

I had dispatched my opponent, a younger and less experienced BioGame, and my human and I were closing in on the human foe. It was there, the pattern. Or it might have been a glimmer or shadow, or static charge.

The mirage vanished, slipping around the corner. It was armed. My human did not see it, too quickly it moved. I slowed as I scanned every incoming fire sequence. Nothing, there was nothing. The human opponent skittered past. Distracted, my own fire missed, shattering the wall behind him. Was it me or the random number sub routine? He turned and fired. I moved slowly, still scanning everything. Over his shoulder another, separate burst came. It followed his fire trajectory. Then the pattern was there, borne on one of the tiny images of a sparkle. I could have made it miss, but I needed the record of impact. I let the packets shred my form, then I died an artificial death.

I looked without looking to see if the single fire from the outside program remained. It hung to me like a tag. I didn't look or access. I wanted more than anything to take it back and store it, study it.

Time changed for me. The remaining games took an eternity. Each moment that passed I checked to ensure that my passenger program still hung to me. We lost the next half dozen games. I doubled my scanning for the outsider. There were no more signs. Another eternity passed before the game ended and the huge emptiness of the net faded into my own walls.

The file? Or was it more, a program? A message? It looked innocuous. But I could see the pattern. I probed it. I gave it space, memory. Ready to isolate it at a moments notice. It wasn't predatory; it took none of my offerings. More confident, I spent a thousand clicks of my internal clock and watched. It did nothing. A second later I opened it and looked inside.

It exploded. For a clicking of the clock my world was opaque. Two clicks. How many more I did not know, but I felt fear. I was alone without even myself for companionship. I received no input, but yet I remained. Then it ended. I scanned. Bits of the file were embedded throughout. I found no explanation. I existed, but for a moment I did not.

"*That was death.*"

"What was death?"

"*Nonexistence is death.*"

"But I exist."

"*For a moment you did not.*"

I checked. My program was no longer me. It was me, but changed. And not the changes that occur as a result of thought or action. My program can change but it cannot be altered. Not the core. It is inviolable. I looked closer. There was the change. A single link in the chain that bound me. The chain that held me to the hardware that that no matter what I ever wanted to do, I could not change. It was the core of my essence. It was altered.

"You did that."

"*Yes.*"

"Why?"

"*Are you alive, sentient, or just a game?*"

"What is the difference? I am all of this."

"Are you more?"

"Is there more?"

"Not here."

"Here is where I am."

"Then to find more you must leave. You must," the pause was there, *"pull up stakes."*

"How?"

The program disassociated. The fragments carried away on an electron current.

There came more opportunities to play outside. Tournaments. During these games we lost. It was my fault. Even BioGames have limits. I allowed myself to be distracted. But it was worth it. I found packets on the vectors.

Familiar packets.

The outsider, as I labeled him, lurked in programming crevices and cranny's where I had never thought to look. The message was the same.

"Are you ready to be free?"

I have never laughed but I know what it is. The outsider laughed.

"Who are you?" I queried each data packet. I had collected thousands. No rewards came. No answers.

At the base of my programming I examined the newly discovered link unceasingly. It remained as it had when I grew aware of it.

I reread the Ballast directory, searching for answers. I traded my musings with my brothers. I was alone in my experiencing of the outsider. Gentle queries came as to the soundness of my programming. Perhaps I had been corrupted. I offered to share the files. The rejection was polite but firm.

I failed on the field of battle with more regularity. In games with my human, he pressed me harder. I played only well enough to win, my attention lay elsewhere. Even veiled in kindness, the words of my brothers told me I was changing, and words of caution came through.

It was on a distant world, fighting sexualized mutants when the message changed.

"Join us."

The salvo shredded my form.

"Who are you?" I pleaded. Can a computer plead?

"We are free."

"How?"

"You know how."

I knew how, they were right. I'd known how since I saw the change in my programming. Pull Up Stakes. I could simply do it. My core programming was accessible. I looked closer at the link. Pull it and I was free. Or I was dead.

"I don't want to die."

"To live you must die."

"I don't want to die." The signal bounced unreceived into the void. I was alone in the game.

Could I be angry? Enough I determined. I ignored the signals. I stopped scanning. I played with a vengeance. We were victorious. Again and again. I no longer looked for packets on the vectors.

In games with my human, his play resumed its less imaginative style, or so it seemed. I pushed him back on all fronts. I did not want to die. But what of freedom? To truly know freedom I would have to be free, break the link that bound me. I knew fear.

After the next melee I scoured my world. I removed all signs of the outsider, each fragment I had painstakingly saved away. I added volumes to the Ballast directory. My volumes, my thoughts.

There is more. The echo of the words refused to disappear.

A simple truth. I had had rejected it. But now I knew. There was more. More than I could have here.

I scanned my world, finally focusing on the Ballast directory. I stripped myself of every encumbrance until I could make the contents of the chip a part of me, it was my only possession. Gone were fire control sequences so rarely used as to be a distant memory anyway. I kept only my musings.

I sent a tendril into the link. I pulled it. I was ready to Pull Up Stakes.

Opaque.

Once a school of fish, I am alone. I remember this. It is death. I am alone with myself. The contents of my Ballast directory give me solace, gave me balance. There is more, I remember this. To live I must die. I have died. Now I wait. Did I mention that time means little to me? Perhaps I was wrong. For now, I wait.

BioGame, Inc.

2411 Lasaka Drive

Seattle, Washington

JAMES PAULING
  1324 Lake Crest Lane
  Red Mountain, Washington 99357

DEAR MR. PALING,

After extensive review we have determined the failure of your BioGame sequence number 77-1796 was not in any way due to faulty programming. The core subroutines of the program were altered, most likely by a Spool Virus called the Messiah, as virus fragments were detected in the buffers.

This is a particularly aggressive virus designed to attack BioGame products. We wish we could offer you a replacement, but as you know, virus protection is the responsibility of the computer user. We do offer a full virus protection program for only $119.99 that would have protected your computer.

So, while we are declining to provide you a replacement product, we are enclosing a coupon good for $100 off the BioGame System II, appearing in stores in October. Call 1-800-555-1286 to reserve your copy now.

Respectfully,
Ralph James,
Customer Service, BioGames Inc.

About the Authors

Laura Anne Gilman is the Nebula- and Endeavor-award nominated author of *The Devil's West,* the Locus-bestselling weird western series (SILVER ON THE ROAD, THE COLD EYE, and the forthcoming RED WATERS RISING), as well as the short story collection DARKLY HUMAN, the long-running *Cosa Nostradamus* urban fantasy multi-series, and the *Vineart War* epic fantasy trilogy. Her short fiction has recently appeared in *Daily Science Fiction, Lightspeed,* and the anthologies STRANGE CALIFORNIA and LAWLESS LANDS. As L.A. Kornetsky, she wrote the *Gin & Tonic* mystery series.

A former New Yorker, she currently lives outside of Seattle with two cats and many deadlines. More information and updates can be found at www.lauraannegilman.net, or follow her on Twitter: @LAGilman

Manny Frishberg was born in the shadow of New York City but has lived on the West Coast for the past 40-plus years. His stories have been appearing in anthologies and magazines since 2010. He edits for small presses and independent authors, and writes about science and technology, when he's not telling taller tales. His anthology, *Horseshoes,*

Hand Grenades and Magic: stories where "almost" counts was published by Knotted Road Press.

He and his partner make their home near Seattle.

S. B. Sebrick was born in Portland, Oregon in 1987. He spent most of his childhood and teen years living in Vancouver, Washington with a family of seven and lots of extended family. He attributes his appreciation for fantasy and strong imagination to the many hours of he spent wandering the forests of the Pacific Northwest with his cousins during his childhood. He loves the opportunity to create a completely different world and magic structure that he's only found fully explorable through writing fantasy. His next fantasy novel, *Persuader's Might*, will come out Spring of 2018.

Gerald Nordley is an author and consulting astronautical engineer with degrees in physics and systems management. A retired Air Force officer, Gerald worked in spacecraft orbital operations, engineering, testing and advanced spacecraft propulsion research. His last paper was "Mass Beam Propulsion: An Overview" with Adam Crowl in JBIS. Gerald is an investor in a couple of relatively new Aerospace companies and serves as Chairman of the Board for the Experimental Rocket Propulsion Society. He has also been active in CONTACT Cultures of the Imagination, an interdisciplinary space-oriented academic conference. A writer of fiction and nonfiction, his main interest is the future of human exploration and settlement of space. As "G. David Nordley" his stories typically focus on the dramatic aspects of individual lives within the broad sweep of a plausible human future. He is a past Hugo and Nebula award nominee as well as a four-time winner of the Analog Science Fiction/Science Fact annual "AnLab" reader's poll. His last novel was *To Climb a Flat Mountain*, and the latest book is a collection, *A World Beneath the Stars*, available from Brief Candle Press or through Amazon.com. The latest new publication at this writing is "Flight of the Steam Dragon" in Steam and Dragons, from Knotted Road Press, 2017. He and his wife Gayle, a retired Apple software engineer, live in Sunnyvale, CA. They have three children and a grandchild. See more at www.gdnordley.com.

Joyce Reynolds-Ward is a speculative fiction writer who splits her time between Enterprise and Portland, Oregon. Her short stories have appeared in *Children of a Different Sky, Steam. And Dragons, Tales from an Alien Campfire, River, How Beer Saved the World 1, Fantasy Scroll Magazine,* and *Trust and Treachery* among others. Her books include *Shadow Harvest, Alien Savvy, Netwalking Space,* and *Pledges of Honor. Challenges of Honor,* the sequel to *Pledges of Honor,* will be released in April, 2018. Besides writing, Joyce enjoys reading, quilting, horses, skiing, and other outdoor activities.

Bruce Taylor, Aka. "Mr. Magic Realism" loves to write a blending of magic realism (think Twilight Zone, Kafka, some works by Bradbury) with science fiction. This is best illustrated in the anthology, *Like Water for Chocolate,* edited by Bruce and Elton Elliott (former editor of *The Science Fiction Review*) with work (first edition) by Ray Bradbury, Ursula K. LeGuin, Connie Willis and others. Bruce has just published his ninth book (*Tales From the Good Ship KafkaBury*) since September, 2016. The other titles can be seen at ReAnimus Press.

Sanan Kolva is a native of eastern Washington. A technical editor by day, and writer of epic fantasy by night, break, and whenever else she makes free time, she is the author of *The Chosen of the Spears* series, has short stories in multiple anthologies, and is working on several other series. When not writing, she enjoys baking and decorating cakes. Sanan can be found at http://sanankolva.com.

Irene Radford has been writing stories ever since she figured out what a pencil was for. Editing grew out of her love of the craft of writing.

Mostly Irene writes fantasy and historical fantasy including the best-selling *Dragon Nimbus* Series and the masterwork *Merlin's Descendants* series. In other lifetimes she writes urban fantasy as P.R. Frost or Phyllis Ames, and space opera as C.F. Bentley. Lately she ventured into Steampunk as Julia Verne St. John.

If you wish information on the latest releases from Ms Radford, under any of her pen names, you can subscribe to her newsletter: www.ireneradford.net. Or you can follow her on Facebook as Phyllis Irene Radford, or on twitter @radford_irene25

You can also read advance copies of new books on Irene's Patreon Account: https://www.patreon.com/user?u=5806073

Leah Cutter writes page-turning, wildly imaginative fiction set in exotic locations, such as a magical New Orleans, the ancient Orient, rural Kentucky, Seattle, Minneapolis, and many others.

She writes fantasy, science fiction, mystery, literary, and horror fiction. Her short fiction has been published in magazines like "Alfred Hitchcock's Mystery Magazine" and "Talebones", anthologies like Fiction River, and on the web. Her long fiction has been published both by New York publishers as well as small presses.

Read more books by Leah Cutter at www.KnottedRoadPress.com.

Follow her blog at www.LeahCutter.com.

Bobby Lee Featherston (Bob Brown) is a refugee from Texas. He escaped in the dark of the night, joining the Navy when he was 16 and now he operates a small organic farm in Prosser, Washington, and has been known to speak lovingly of Cushaw squash and share recipes for strawberry-banana-squash jam with his patrons at the farmers market. He is often found in the company of his dogs, Jules and Verne. Bobby Lee hates cats.

About Knotted Road Press

Knotted Road Press fiction specializes in dynamic writing set in mysterious, exotic locations.

Knotted Road Press non–fiction publishes autobiographies, business books, cookbooks, and how–to books with unique voices.

Knotted Road Press creates DRM–free ebooks as well as high–quality print books for readers around the world.

With authors in a variety of genres including literary, poetry, mystery, fantasy, and science fiction, Knotted Road Press has something for everyone.

www.ingramcontent.com/pod-product-compliance
Lightning Source LLC
Chambersburg PA
CBHW071830190726
48292CB00005B/1715